LARK

LARK

Tracey Porter

Laura Geringer Books

Lark

Copyright © 2011 by Tracey Porter

All rights reserved. Printed in the United States of America.

No part of this book may be used or reproduced in any manner

whatsoever without written permission except in the case of brief quotations

embodied in critical articles and reviews. For information address

HarperCollins Children's Books, a division of HarperCollins Publishers,

10 East 53rd Street, New York, NY 10022.

www.epicreads.com

Library of Congress Cataloging-in-Publication Data

Porter, Tracey.

    Lark / Tracey Porter. — 1st ed.

        p.   cm.

    Summary: When sixteen-year-old Lark is murdered, she, her childhood best friend, Eve, and a girl she used to babysit, Nyetta, find themselves facing hard truths about their lives and seeking a way to move on.

    ISBN 978-0-06-112287-3

    [1. Interpersonal relations—Fiction. 2. Murder—Fiction. 3. Grief—Fiction. 4. Family life—Virginia—Fiction. 5. Supernatural—Fiction. 6. Arlington (Va.)—Fiction.] I. Title.

PZ7.P83395Lar 2011   2010021959

[Fic]—dc22   CIP

                                                  AC

Typography by Carla Weise

11 12 13 14 15 CG/RRDB 10 9 8 7 6 5 4 3 2 1

❖

First Edition

Dedicated to the memory of
Tasha Semler
(1959–1973)
and
Catherine Schilling
(1959–1981)

1. *Nyetta*

First he hit her, then he stabbed her with a small knife, but Lark didn't die from this. She died from the cold. She was naked, and he tied her to a tree so she wouldn't run away. He left her there uncovered, and the storm came and she died because it was too cold to live through the night. The police found her in the woods near my house. The story was in the paper. My mother took it away from me, but I found it in her desk cut out and folded under envelopes and string.

Since then I've had trouble sleeping. I keep the light on, but even then I'm still afraid, so my mother reads her book in the chair in my room. If I can't close my eyes, she crawls into my bed and holds me till I sleep.

Lark wants me to see her. She needs me to see where the knife went in, because if no one knows what it was like for her, then her spirit will be trapped in that tree. I've read about girls like this, the ones who live in trees. Every part of them changes to wood but the heart. Their fingers and hair turn into leaves. Their arms become branches. There is not much time left.

Sometimes I hear her.

"Look," she says, spreading her hands. The tips of her fingers are blue from the cold. Her hair glistens with ice. She starts to lift her dress, but I tell her to stop.

"I can't," I say.

"Oh," she says, then turns away. It's easy for her to come and go right now, but it won't be for long.

She doesn't want to scare me, but she can't bear being trapped in that tree.

2. Eve

The last time I saw Lark, it was almost dark. She was limping up the driveway with a brace on her knee and a huge bag over her shoulders. Her hair was clipped in a twist. I was at my desk, drawing a windmill in a field scattered with leaves. Some were like crumpled stars, others like hands. I drew them tiny and distinct, each one the size of a dime. I knocked on the glass, and Lark looked up and waved. I thought she looked tired. Maybe her knee was hurting.

That was weeks ago. Days later, she went missing. My parents called me into their room to tell me. The news was on, but the TV was mute.

"Lark's father just called," said my dad, still holding the phone. "He wanted to know if you knew where she is."

"No . . ." I was annoyed. I had a chem lab to finish.

"She wasn't at the gym when her father went to pick her up," he explained.

"And?" I asked

"Her parents thought you might know where she is."

"No idea." I shrugged.

"Does she have a boyfriend?" my mom asked. Her face was puckered, like she was trying to keep something inside.

"Not that I know of. But that doesn't mean anything. I haven't talked to her in a while."

"Sometimes girls share things they wouldn't tell their parents," my mom said.

"No." I shook my head. "Lark and I haven't been close in a long time."

Outside it was snowing. Huge flakes fell thick and heavy. I think about that night in drawings, little squares of a story—Lark with a brace on her knee, me at my window, my parents talking to me from their bed, snow falling, the tree by the river.

The next day at school, a circle of girls gathered outside of World Civ. "She probably ran away after a fight with her parents," said Alyssa.

"Maybe she's with some guy she met online," said Beth, Alyssa's best friend.

I know Alyssa from the swim team, back when I used to swim. She's tall, still a serious swimmer, drowning in her boyfriend's letter jacket.

"She wouldn't do that," I said. "I know her. She's my neighbor."

"Well, I know her too," said Beth. She flipped her Goldilocks hair and glared at me. "She was my sister's best friend until she got so obsessed with gymnastics."

"Did the police question you?" asked Alyssa. "I heard they went to every house on her street."

"No."

With this I became less interesting. If I had lied, the circle would have opened for me. But I don't lie.

The bell rang, then the new girl from Boston stepped in front of me. She's clumsy and chatty, long curly brown hair parted in the middle. Alyssa and Beth find her accent hysterical. In class, they goad her to ask questions so they can crack up.

"She's probably been kidnapped," said Boston, chewing her gum. "By a serial killer."

A hush fell. Alyssa blinked. My stomach fluttered and jumped, like a bird was trapped inside. And then

Mr. Haus put his head out the doorway and told us to come in. He wasn't angry, so I figured he knew about Lark.

In class, everyone was quiet and well behaved. No one texted or played Tetris or whispered to a friend. Mr. Haus pointed to the Tigris and the Euphrates on the frayed map. Some kids asked questions, and all of us took notes. In the margins of my notes, I drew a circle of girls. Girls talking and listening. One clutching her binder. Another holding her hand to her mouth, afraid. I couldn't concentrate. I kept thinking about what Boston said and how she was probably right.

Girls who go missing for more than a few hours are usually found dead. Three summers ago, in different parts of the country, two girls went missing the same week. One was riding her bike home from a friend's house. The other was taken through her bedroom window. Their school portraits smiled at us from the magazine racks in grocery stores. Our mothers turned off the news when we walked into the kitchen. They didn't want us to know about things like this yet. I bet every girl in my high school remembers that summer. In the end, the girls were found dead, both killed by men who had already been in jail.

Two days later, Lark was found dead. Her parents called mine and told them she was found in the woods near our street, the same woods we used to explore when we were best friends. Since then, I've been waiting for something to happen, some kind of meeting or conference where all kinds of experts get together to figure out why this sort of thing keeps happening to girls. I keep wondering if the police have put up a warning sign in the woods.

MISSING GIRL FOUND DEAD

―◄◦►―

JANUARY 25: The body of a 16-year-old Arlington girl missing since last Monday was found yesterday in a heavily wooded area of Potomac Overlook Park. Medical examiners report the girl had been beaten and stabbed, but the likely cause of death was exposure. The girl had been tied to a tree, then left during the night of the area's first major snowstorm.

Lark Austin was reported missing when she disappeared after her gymnastics lesson at the Virginia Gymnastics Academy. She was last seen getting into a dark car heading north on Lee Highway.

3. Lark

I was tired, leaning against the glass door, wondering when it was finally going to snow, waiting for my father to pick me up. I shifted my weight, trying to find how to stand so my knee wouldn't hurt.

My coach saw me wince after I dismounted the beam. I wanted to go on, but he made me sit on the bench. I iced my knee, watching the other girls practice, my stomach in knots. I'd have to see the orthopedist and go back to physical therapy. I'd have to ice it every night and wear my brace. Even then I might not be able to compete in regionals. The night I died, I had an essay to finish and a physics test to study for. I was planning to be up past midnight, studying and writing and taking care of my knee.

A black car pulled up. The driver rolled down the window and gestured me over. I thought he was the father of one of the younger girls. His face was shiny and pink, like he scrubbed it with a rough cloth.

"I need help," he said. His breath turned white in the air. "My kid's in the ER. Oh, he's awful messed up. Got hit by a car riding his skateboard. I just got the call."

He was fast talking and frantic. He kept looking from me to his overhead mirror. The light was on. A map was spread out on the front seat.

"You know where the hospital is?"

"I'm not really sure. . . ."

"The cop said it's on Lee Highway."

"I think it's over that away. . . ." I pointed far down the road to the next intersection.

"That's what I thought, too, but it isn't. Can you look at this map, please? Can you show me Lee Highway? Please, miss. You seem like a nice person. I gotta get to the hospital. My kid might not make it."

I let my bag fall to the sidewalk and went over to his car. He opened the door.

"Oh, thank you," he said when I sat down. I picked up the map and turned it around, then he reached across me and slammed the door. He took off so fast, I was flung back in the seat.

"Hey!" I yelled. "What are you doing?"

"I need to get to the hospital."

"Stop!" I yelled. "Let me out!"

He kept driving, saying, "You need to help me find the hospital," and when I said I had to call my dad, he gave me his phone but the battery was dead.

4. Nyetta

Lark's ghost is lonely and sad, not like she was in real life. In real life, laughter burst out of her like soda does when you shake the can. She'd flick her ponytail from one shoulder to the other, then dart her eyes into yours to tell you a joke.

When my dad left, she used to babysit me so my mom could work in her office. She liked our backyard because it's spongy and smooth. She showed me her floor routine with the handspring and splits. She taught me to cartwheel and pivot, and how to kick up to a handstand against the wall. She gave me my own set of ribbons and taught me how to make them spiral. She loved ice skating and ballet, gymnastics and diving. "Anything with form," she said, putting her head on her knees and pointing her toes, like when you do a jackknife. She called it pike position. It was gymnastics she loved best.

"Kick your legs open," she told me. "Like you're doing the splits."

I was running in leaps across the backyard, spiraling the ribbons, kicking my legs as much as I could, only my front leg collapsed and I fell like a rag doll.

Lark fell over laughing. "You're like me! More flexible than strong."

She said we have to be careful or else we'll get injured.

"We've got to work our core," she said, and then

she showed me the right way to do sit-ups and told me not to worry about stretching so much.

Between visits I did my sit-ups and practiced my spirals. But then she went to high school, and she didn't have time to babysit me anymore. She had AP classes and practice, competitions and science projects, newspaper deadlines and physical therapy for her bad knee.

"You'll see," my mother said. "You'll be that busy when you're her age."

How awful, I thought.

Now I'm too old for a babysitter when my mom works at home, only I don't like being alone.

I wish I were braver.

Lark is drifting around those woods, frightened that the tree will take her inside forever. All I have to do to save her is look.

5. *Eve*

There are secret paths all over my neighborhood, trails of crushed leaves and beaten grass. The animals follow them—wild ones and pets, raccoons and badgers and everyone's dogs. The paths are narrow, almost hidden. We hear about them from the teenage girls who babysit or from someone's big brother. We trade information at block parties, gathering in someone's basement, while our parents drink martinis. The trails lead from one backyard to another, through the old woods near Overlook Pool and Recreation Center. They follow creeks and lead between boulders, ending at the cliff above the river.

The last summer we were friends, Lark and I explored the path from the pool to the cliff. There was a secret place, a fallen tree where you could sit and see the river, that we wanted to find. She was thirteen and I was twelve. We took the fork that led to the river instead of the one that emptied in the cul-de-sac by our street. Our swimsuits were still damp. We tucked our towels under the straps so they hung down our backs like capes. Our flip-flops left ridged prints in the mud. Birds flitted to the water and drank. A flash of red was a cardinal; yellow, an oriole. There were catbirds and hummingbirds, chickadees, too. I learned all the birds from handouts at the nature center when I was little. I colored them so furiously I picked up the grain from the picnic table.

The trail leads behind the new subdivision my dad designed. We smelled the sap oozing from fences in the summer heat. We heard the sounds of families and barbecues. Big Wheels on decks. Bags of ice emptying into coolers. The fizz of soda poured into cups. Sloshing through the creek in the culvert, we scraped a stick against the corrugated tin, the circle of light ahead of us tinged with green.

Once we were out the other side, the trail ended and our neighborhood disappeared. It was like being in a spell cast by a good witch. Generations of fallen leaves gathered against tree trunks and saplings. The ground was loamy and soft as felt. We walked stealthy and silent on the outside of our feet because we didn't want to scare the animals away. They watched us from tree limbs and burrows—stern, silent owls and a family of foxes, a bobcat twitching the black tip of its tail.

Hundreds of feet below us, the Potomac rumbled

and roared. We crept along the edge until we found the huge tree the teenagers told us about, a sycamore struck by lightning that had started to roll down the cliff years ago. It was moss covered and hollow, trapped by the roots and trunks of other trees. We sat there and looked out to the three tiny islands in the middle of the river.

They're called the Three Sisters. The river swirls and eddies around them. One has a tree growing in the middle. They're named after three Indian princesses who ran away from home. Their father wanted to marry off the oldest one to a chief in another village, but the sisters loved one another too much to be separated. So they begged the river god to hide their footsteps and let them pass. He agreed, but since he was cruel and they were beautiful, he turned them into three small islands to keep for himself.

That day the noise of the river smothered our voices. We had to yell to hear ourselves, but we wanted the animals to stay with us, so we stopped talking. We took turns throwing stones into the river, trying to reach the islands, trying to say hello to the three Indian girls. We dug past layers of crinkly leaves and dry dirt to the damp soil where the stones were buried. They were rough and gray just like the islands. The stones arced through the air, past the farthest branches of the most far-leaning trees, disappearing once they left our hands. Sometimes they streamed past the canopy of branches, and for a moment we saw them sailing through a patch of blue sky.

Later that summer, something bad happened to me. I tried telling Lark, but she wouldn't listen and my mom asked the wrong questions. I buried it deep inside me, like the rough stones we found under the leaves.

6. *Lark*

My legs were shaking and my heart was pounding so hard, I felt the pulse in my ears.

"Let me out! Let me out! Let me out!" I cried. I banged on the window, trying to get the attention of the driver in the next lane, but the windows were tinted black and no one could see me.

"Please," I begged. I was sobbing now. "Please let me go." But he didn't answer. He stared at the road, silent and inexpressive like he was carved out of stone.

He took the parkway to Washington, the one without streetlights that cuts through the woods. He turned onto a dark road that I had seen many times but had never been on. It ended in a parking lot used by maintenance crews and road workers. He parked behind a snowplow and zipped the keys in his pocket. He spoke in a soft voice like he was trying to sound kind.

"I've been watching you for a long time. You're special to me.

"I don't want to hurt you. I only want to get to know you better."

The air in the car seemed to expand and get thin. It was like being inside a balloon as it was being blown up. My body was only heartbeat and breath. The car was metal and glass. The man was his face. My hands weren't even there.

The man said, "I'm going to tie your hands now, so I can keep you safe."

Somewhere inside me a firm, quiet voice spoke up. *You know these woods,* it said. *If you get away from him, you can find the path to your house and he won't be able to catch you. Make him think you're too scared to escape.*

"No," I said. "You don't have to. I'll go with you."

Then I got sick, but since I hadn't eaten anything since lunch there was nothing to throw up but water and bile. He picked up a rag from the floor and wiped my face.

"See," he said, "nothing bad is going to happen."

The man reached around to the backseat. I watched him lean over and twist. I heard him grunt with the effort because he was fat. I heard him push the rag under the rubber mat. I waited until he had turned around as far as he could, then I opened the door and ran.

7. *Nyetta*

My mother says I have to start going back to school, only I can't because I'm too tired and I don't really want to see anyone or leave the house.

"It seems that both of you are interested in the dead," says Dr. Huber when my mom tells him why I'm not sleeping. He's always liked that she's an archaeologist. Now that she's divorced, I bet he asks her out.

My mother answers a lot of questions. Pale sunlight drifts through the window. He's talking loudly, like he wants me to join the conversation, but I don't. Instead I study the dust motes floating in the air. I'm small for twelve, the smallest girl in the seventh grade. It occurs to me that I'm growing smaller. Soon, I may even disappear. This might be a good thing.

Dr. Huber talks mostly to my mother. For a second, I feel like telling him that I am absolutely not interested in the dead, that I couldn't care less about them, and that what interests me is trees and how girls turn into them if people forget or don't know, or if no one finds the person who hurt them.

The urge to speak passes. Dr. Huber doesn't seem very interested anyway. He doesn't want to know what Lark says, or how she is being very patient and very gentle, even though she is disappointed that I can't look at her.

He takes my temperature and pulse. Then he looks in my throat and takes blood.

"I'll call you with the results," he tells my mother, "but most likely it's anxiety, caused by the trauma of your neighbor's death. Let's give it some time and hold off on medication."

In the meantime, he tells her to give me chamomile tea and have me listen to a relaxation CD she can buy at the bookstore.

"And she should probably see a therapist," he says. "Someone Nyetta can talk to so she can get back to her life at school and being with friends."

Being with friends. I can almost remember it, the way I remember playing with dolls.

8. *Eve*

"Are you sure you want to go to school today?" asks my mom. She's worried because I haven't cried about Lark. I'm on autopilot. I've been like this for a long time, only she hasn't noticed.

I have lots of little secrets from my parents. They don't know about the stacks of drawings under my bed or the Van Gogh pictures I've cut out from their art books and taped inside my closet door. They would complain I've ruined books, but they'll never notice. They haven't looked at an art book in years. They don't know how much I know about pen and ink, how you build an image line by line without blending, only short lines or long, no room for error. If you hold the pen too firmly, the ink bleeds over the image. If you hold it too lightly, your line is insubstantial and weak. Which is one of the many reasons I love Vincent van Gogh. I've studied his sketchbooks and read all his letters to his brother Theo. He never missed a beat.

My parents are both artists, or used to be. I don't consider what they do now as art. They want me to be a lawyer.

"But, honey," says my mom. "You look *so* tired. Don't you want a day off?"

I tell her I have to go to school, that I can't possibly miss World Civ because Mr. Haus is reviewing for the test and there's an in-class essay in English. All this is true. She bites her lip and sends me on my way. Inside my binder I've taped a drawing of a man carrying a lantern. Van Gogh drew it in the margins of a letter to Theo. I can't figure out how he made it light up the dark.

The air is crystalline and brittle. I have a new superfine pen from Japan in my purse. The wind whips my coat around my legs. I wrap my scarf over my mouth and nose so I don't breathe in the cold. I trudge through the slush to Thomas Jefferson High, home of the Rebels.

I'd forgotten it's the day of the big game against our archrival, Washington-Lee. A wave of team spirit pushes me through the front door. People rush to get a better view of the pep parade marching through the hall. Cheerleaders shake their pompoms and bounce. The marching band steps high, tilting their instruments and blaring the fight song. In between the band members, the basketball team cruises along. People jostle and push. My new pen falls out of my bag and rolls across the floor.

The band finishes to big applause and several rounds of "Go Rebels! Kill Generals!" Then the five-minute bell rings and everyone scatters. Cheerleaders stuff pom-poms in lockers. Skaters and stoners lift their fists in mock school spirit and slink off to class. Behind me, two boys are talking about Lark.

"Pretty cold," says one.

"What do you mean?" asks the other.

"Having a pep rally so soon after Lark Austin was found dead."

I turn around to see a junior named Ian. He writes music reviews for the paper. I recognize him from the photo by his column. He catches my glance, then drops his eyes to the floor. He seems embarrassed or shy. The crowd thins, and I spy my pen under the drinking fountain. I slip it into my bag and rush off to class.

The day goes on, simultaneously numbing and exhausting. For the second year in a row I didn't get

Studio Art, my first choice for electives. Instead I have Debate with Ms. Curren. She assigns us to topics and teams. I'm placed on the side against stem cell research, with Darren and Scott, two boys who live for basketball, and Judith, an honors student with short hair and ennui. We push our desks together, then I pull out my binder and start drawing Van Gogh's traveler carrying a lantern in the dark. All three of them, I am surprised to learn, are in the Animal Rights Club.

"Why?" I ask, noticing Judith's huge leather purse.

"Because it's an easy way to get your community service experience," says Scott. He moves his hands when he talks, like he's spinning a record. "You bake some brownies for a bake sale, go to the shelter, walk the dogs around the block, and *bam!* You're looking good for college!"

"Colleges love animal rights," agrees Judith. "That's how my sister got into Bard. She was president of the club in her senior year."

Darren is unhappy about our assignment. "Hey, Mizz Curren!" he yells. He lifts his elbows and taps his chest when he talks. He's so animated, the chain on his wallet jingles. "We're all for stem cell research, you know, to help the babies and all the folks with bad hearts and diabetes. We can't debate against it!"

Ms. Curran nods empathetically. "Yes, Darren, it can be a challenge to develop an argument for a position you *deeply* oppose. But in the long run, nothing will help you defend your ideas more effectively than learning how to compose an argument for the other side."

"See, bro," says Scott, "that's what I told you she'd say."

Darren takes off his cap and turns it around. Judith checks her nails. I'm filling in the man's coat with crosshatching. Ink flows from my pen, drenching the paper, smearing the lines. I'm off. If Darren and

Scott would shut up, I'd control the pen better.

Hours tick by. Between classes I clutch my binder and edge through the crowd. In algebra, I will myself right back into the man's walk in the night, rays of his lantern piercing the darkness.

Finally the last bell rings. Everyone's pumped up, making plans about who's driving to the game, who's having an after party, and which one is worth going to. The marching band assembles at the flagpole, playing "Hit Me Baby One More Time," keeping spirits high until game time. The blare of the trombones and beat of the drums make me nauseated. Alyssa, Boston, and Beth are in attendance, yelling, "Kill Generals! Kill Generals! Kill Generals!" at the top of their lungs. They imitate the cheerleaders and fall over themselves laughing, Alyssa because she's too good of an athlete to take cheerleaders seriously, Boston and Beth because Alyssa's their queen.

I come home to NPR blasting through the

speakers my dad installed last Christmas. I dump my books on the window seat and wander into the kitchen. My parents are busy in their studios. Mom, part owner of Hand-Made ceramics gallery, is busy at the wheel, throwing teapots. Dad's color coordinating tiles and countertops for a huge house that's trying to look like Mount Vernon. The developer cut down fourteen trees to build it. It has a great room, a spiral staircase, and a four-car garage. When Dad showed me the plans, I told him he had sold his soul.

"And it's ugly. With a huge carbon footprint," I said. "No one will buy it in this economy."

"Let's hope you're wrong," he said. "Your college tuition depends on it."

I've been overhearing my parents talk about money. They sit at the breakfast table with the laptop and stacks of bills. We're overextended, they say. My mom's store might close, and my dad has only one project going, not like the days when he and

Mr. McCall built the town houses near the pool.

Somewhere behind the blueprints of all the McMansions and the subdivisions are my dad's old canvases and paints. He used to paint landscapes. There's a shelf of glass jars with perfect lids, the ones that you shake to blend tertiary paints. By now the pigments must be dried and cracked. One drop of water would turn them back into paint.

My dad emerges from his studio, well meaning and quizzical. "How was school?" he asks.

"We had a pep rally," I say, putting the kettle on for tea.

"No kidding," he says, sounding shocked. "Well . . . I suppose it's best to get things back to normal."

"Whatever normal is," I say. It seems girls getting kidnapped and murdered is fairly normal. The window above the sink is edged in frost. I touch it with my fingertip, enjoying the slight burn.

9. *Lark*

The air was brittle and cold. My teeth chattered. I ran across the asphalt into the woods. The sky broke open and snowflakes fell around me like dying moths.

I didn't get far. Each step sent shockwaves of pain to my knee. I slipped and fell facedown in the snow. I got up, but I couldn't get enough traction to get any speed. The man was right behind me. He grabbed me around the waist and flung me to the ground. He crawled over me and slugged the side of my face with his fist. He took something out of his pocket and flicked it open.

"You made me do this," he said, pushing a knife between my ribs. Its point cut through my jacket and touched my skin. He started to cry. "I didn't want to do this, but you made me."

At first it felt like a pencil point. Then it stung. Then it felt like fire, and the pain stopped my breath. I was afraid to move because I thought the knife would go into my heart.

10. *Nyetta*

I'm sleeping when Lark rattles the window and lets herself in. Moonlight fills my room with silvery light. She wears the flowing white dress she was buried in. She could be a sylph in a ballet, except for the bloodstains.

"So . . . , " she says. "They think you're crazy."

I rub my eyes and yawn. "Well, I am acting rather oddly."

"How?"

"Talking to a dead girl. Not sleeping. Not going to school."

Lark rolls her eyes. "School!" she says with disgust. "I worried way too much about school."

She's restless. She taps her foot angrily.

"I won't tell them how I have to see the cut," I say.

"If you do, they'll try to talk you out of it."

"I know."

She flops in my armchair and props up her head with a fist.

"I hate it out there," she says.

"I know," I say.

"No, you don't. Believe me. You don't."

Her eyes fill with tears, the kind of tears you get when you're angry and sad. She rocks back and forth, softly crying. Then she shakes herself out of it and jumps up to move. She practices one of her floor routines, the one with the back flips that won her a medal. She's got that twitchy energy back. She's alive again, thinking with her body, the way dancers and athletes do. Even though her movements are small and contained, you can tell how good she was. She uses her hands for the big tricks, like the round off to a twisting back flip. She marks the big leaps, fitting them in between the furniture and the walls.

I watch Lark remember how she used to cartwheel and flip. She tosses her head and laughs to herself. She arches her back and finishes, her hands high above her head. It's scary to know a girl as fast and strong as Lark can get taken away and killed.

11. *Eve*

Days pass. Speculation about who killed Lark and why subsides, and the girls in World Civ are back to texting and playing Tetris. One morning out of the blue, our first-period teacher tells us we're having a special assembly. The entire school piles into the gym to see Principal Akers at a podium, surrounded by a small army of strangers carrying clipboards and briefcases. He tells us the deans have set up special tables with art supplies in the library where we can make cards and drawings and write poems.

"Honor roll student, dedicated athlete, Lark Austin was one of the students who make us proud to be a part of Thomas Jefferson High."

A freshman girl starts shaking and crying. The old government teacher who always wears a bow tie and has been around so long he's taught some of our parents wipes his eyes. A row down from me, a couple leans together. The boy puts his arm around the girl, and I wonder why I can't cry or feel something like sadness. After all, we grew up together. She used to be my best friend.

Principal Akers goes on.

"The people you see with me are grief counselors, professionally trained therapists that our wonderful PTA has brought here to help us process our feelings about the terrible tragedy that befell Lark."

He says they'll be visiting health classes, and that he and the deans are here for us at this difficult time.

"Did you see the young one?" asks Boston, edging through the crowd to be near Alyssa. "I like his fauxhawk."

"Yeah," answers Beth. "I hope he comes to our class." But he doesn't. Instead, Ms. Sims introduces Kate Battle, a licensed social worker who specializes in grief work with young people.

"I'm a retired policewoman, too," adds Kate, "and I'm here to help you to grieve and to give you some tips about how to keep safe. We're going to be talking and sharing, so the first thing I want you to do is make yourselves comfortable."

Girls stretch out on the floor or prop up their heads on their desks. Boston takes her place in the front next to Beth and Alyssa. I sit down cross-legged in the corner of the room. I'm angry, but I don't know why. I pull out my sketchbook and start drawing cypress trees and clouds.

Kate Battle uses her hands when she talks. "The most important thing you can learn from me today," she says, "is how to stay safe. So before we talk about the terrible thing that happened to your classmate, let's go over a list of tips I've prepared for you."

She asks for a volunteer to distribute the handouts, and Boston jumps up. Kate Battle goes on. "Read silently, please, as I go over the list. . . ."

I place the handout on my sketchbook and look it over.

Avoid being alone.

Men who are predators will first try to gain your trust.

If they think you're easily pushed around, they'll move in.

Never be afraid to be rude. Do not worry about hurting a stranger's feelings if you are uncomfortable.

If a man who is bothering you doesn't go away, say "Get away from me NOW!" in a loud voice.

Try not to smile or laugh out of nervousness. Try not to act "cute."

If you must walk or wait alone, never wear headphones. Many victims are abducted or attacked because they don't hear the man sneaking up on them.

Carry your keys so they stick out between your knuckles and can be used as a weapon.

Kate Battle demonstrates how to rake someone's face with her own keys. But I only have one key since I don't drive yet. Not much of a weapon. Besides, how can you really tell if a guy is all right or a sex offender? And aren't girls supposed to be nice? Aren't we supposed to let the guy make the first move?

Ms. Sims asks if anyone would like to ask our guest speaker a question or share some feelings. One girl says how she didn't know Lark personally, but she thinks that what happened to her is really, really sad. Another girl says something like it happened to her cousin's best friend in Pennsylvania. Boston tells the story of a girl at her sister's old high school who was killed by a drunk driver on her way home from the prom. But since it doesn't have anything to do with what happened to Lark, Alyssa and Beth burst out laughing.

"You are *so* random!" laughs Alyssa.

It takes a while before Ms. Sims can restore order. She tells them they either have to stop laughing or leave.

"We're okay, we're okay . . . ," Alyssa protests. "Please, don't kick us out. This is a really good class. We don't want to leave."

"Well, then act like it," orders Ms. Sims.

The girls calm down and pretend to be serious. I go back to my drawing, half listening to stories about girls who've been abducted or assaulted. Surprisingly, no one mentions Daphne, the girl who left school. Last winter she passed out drunk at a party. Her friends walked her into one of the bedrooms, and a little while later a couple of guys went in and raped her. Her parents pressed charges and sued the host's parents for letting underage kids drink at their house. But most people blamed Daphne for what happened because she wore too much makeup and was always getting wasted. Apparently none of her friends stood up for her. She got depressed and her parents dropped the suit. So I guess Daphne broke the rules by being alone in the bedroom, but maybe her friends broke them by leaving her alone when she couldn't take care of herself. Or maybe she acted cute when those guys came in, which is something Kate Battle says you should never, ever do if you have even the tiniest thought that a guy could be a predator. Maybe Daphne laughed or did something that made the guys think she wanted to have sex with them. In the end, she lost all her friends and dropped out to get homeschooled. The guys weren't even suspended. They said it was consensual.

In my corner, I'm drawing a swirling cypress tree. Branches curl and lift as I sift through the details. Some things fall between categories, like what happened to me with the assistant swim coach when I was twelve. Boston raises her hand.

"Was Lark raped?" she asks.

"Detectives aren't saying," says Kate Battle.

"Why not?" says Alyssa.

"Sometimes police keep evidence secret until it's been verified by a lab so it can be used in questioning the suspect."

"Why?" asks Jess.

"Usually when there's a murder, the only living witness is the murderer. If we tell the press we've found scraps of fabric or lint on the victim or at the scene the crime, the killer might read it. Then, if we pick him up for questioning, he will have had the chance to get rid of something that might link him to the crime."

"And then, of course, there's sperm," announces Alyssa. "You can tell a guy's blood type from sperm."

Girls groan in disgust, me included. Boston shows Beth something she's written on her hand and they both giggle.

"And there's something else," says the grief counselor, "that all of you in this room should know. It's about how you dress and how you move and how you walk. You're young women now, and how you conduct yourself gives off signals, whether you like it or not."

Alyssa jerks up her head and rolls her eyes at Kate. "Yeah, right," she says. "As if Lark wore a tank top to gymnastics because she wanted to be killed."

For once I agree with Alyssa. I put down my pen and listen to Kate Battle's response.

"No, of course not," counters Kate, "but at the same time, it's important to be aware that you are not just powerless victims. There are things you can do to prevent things like this."

I don't know about that. I'm starting to believe in luck as the ruling power.

Outside, the world goes on in its usual way. From where I'm sitting, I can look out the window onto the street. A bus goes by, then a truck carrying huge spools of wire. People run to a store or get coffee or take a package to the post office. Kate Battle urges us to keep talking and processing. Then she asks Boston to help her pass out a flyer for the girls-only self-defense class she teaches on Saturdays.

Suddenly, I realize why I've been angry all period. None of this is about Lark. People have stopped thinking about her. They're taking the lessons they need and moving on. And the grief counselor, who came to help us process our feelings, is trying to drum up a little business for herself.

"No, thank you," I tell Boston when she offers me the flyer.

Boston smiles at me and snaps her gum.

12. *Lark*

His hands clawed at my clothes, pulling them off with the hooks of his fingers. He pinned my arms with his knees and took off his pants. I begged him to stop. I told him I was a virgin, but he didn't care.

He forced himself into me, and that's when I stopped feeling what was happening. I willed myself far away so it was almost like sleeping.

He couldn't stay hard, so he slapped me and called me a slut and said that he should have known what I was. Not a girl he could love but a slut like the others. Then he tried again but he couldn't stay inside, so he yelled at me again, then he came on my leg.

He lay on top of me for a long time before he pushed himself off.

"Get up," he said, but I couldn't move. I lay there with the snow falling on my face, looking up to the sky.

"Get up!" he yelled. He saw the blood on his hands and started to cry. "You made me do this. I never wanted to hurt you! Oh, no! Oh, no!"

He kept saying he was so sorry, that he could tell I was a good girl after all and that he would help me. He said he'd come right back, but that he couldn't trust me, so he dragged me to a tree and tied my arms behind my back with plastic ties. They cut into my wrists. I was too weak to stand. When I fell, the bark scraped my skin. My bad knee twisted and I heard the ligament tear. It sounded like fabric when you rip it in half.

I heard him run through the snow and his car start. Wind whooshed through the trees but couldn't lift my hair because it was starting to freeze. Each breath seemed to open the wound in my side a little bit more. I was so cold, I decided to die. It was easy. Like stepping out of your clothes when they fall to the floor.

I hovered over my body, watching the snow fall on my neck, studying the horrible bend in my knee.

Then the dead girls spoke to me.

Don't look, said one.

Turn away, said another.

Come over here, said the third.

Their bodies were trapped in their trees. I saw faces under the bark.

It's almost over . . . , said the one keeping watch. *Now.*

She closed her eyes and began to cry. Snow turned to sleet and covered the branches in ice.

Off in the distance I died.

13. *Nyetta*

My therapist, Dr. Blake, has an office filled with toys that are way too young for me. She wears glasses and a gypsy skirt and a huge sweater that must belong to her husband. I think she's been a hippie most of her life. I'm supposed to call her April, not Dr. Blake.

"Can you tell me about your friend who died?" asks April. She adjusts her glasses and smiles.

I'm fiddling with the clay she gave me, pushing it into a pot, then flattening it out and starting over again. I don't really like talking about Lark, but she keeps trying to force me.

"How did you know her?" she tries again.

"She lived down the street," I say.

"What was she like?" she asks.

She's persistent; I'll say that for her. She's not about to stop asking me questions. My mom says I've got to try to say what I'm feeling, only I'm not feeling anything, except sort of jumpy at night when I think Lark might be coming.

"She used to babysit me. After my father left. But then she stopped and then she died."

I've formed the clay into a perfect little pinch pot. If I had a bird, I'd put the bowl in its cage for water.

"Tell me about your father," she says.

"My father doesn't live with us anymore," I answer. "He lives with Hallie."

It's much easier to talk about my father than Lark, so I tell April the whole story—how Hallie used to work for my dad at the museum, how they fell in love, how my dad left my mom and moved in with Hallie and her sons. Their names are Anders and Zeke. They're twins. Age eight. Noisy. Sometimes I run into my dad and the twins when I'm out with my mom. They play football in the park and buy rockets at the hobby store. Zeke's hair is so curly, it bounces.

"And how does it make you feel?" asks April. "Seeing your dad playing with the boys? Knowing he left to go live with another family?"

I smash the bowl with my fingers.

"Well . . . ," I start. I decide to speak with long pauses between all the important words, which is what some grown-ups do when they're angry. April leans forward to encourage me. Her big hippie skirt has spread to a half circle on the floor.

"I used . . . to feel . . . sad. But now . . . I don't . . . care."

"Why not?"

"Because it's better if people are happy. If Hallie makes my dad happy, then he should be with her. Then he will be a better father for me."

"That sounds like a thought, not a feeling."

"I like thoughts. They're better than feelings."

This ends up being a stupid thing to admit. April takes a few notes on her yellow pad, which is a sign that she's about to zero in on something.

She puts her pencil down. "All right then. Thoughts it is. I want to get back to Lark before we have to go. Where do you think she is?"

"She's not really anywhere," I answer. "She's dead."

"Your mom tells me you talk to her sometimes."

I'm peering down at my clay, studying how it captures my fingerprints. I'm going to let this one pass.

"Do you believe in an afterlife?" April asks.

I believe in trees, I think. But I would never say this out loud. I promised myself I wouldn't tell April about trees unless she specifically asks, which she never will. How many people know about dead girls and trees?

I decide not to talk for the rest of the session. Instead I play with the clay.

The clock ticks. Dr. Blake watches me but doesn't ask any more questions.

"All right then," she says finally. "See you next week."

14. *Eve*

His name was Trevor; he was the son of my father's partner, although I didn't know him before he was my swim coach. When Mr. Landis announced that he was going to be his assistant coach, Alyssa and the other kids who knew him broke out in cheers. His trophies gleamed behind a glass cabinet on the Dolphin Wall of Champions. At sixteen, he set a county record for the 100-meter butterfly. Two years later he won a swimming scholarship to the University of Virginia. His family owned a big piece of land next to the pool with a two-hundred-year-old house that looked like something out of *Gone with the Wind*. It was set back from the road, framed by old trees with tall twisting branches. My dad said the McCalls used to own all the land in our neighborhood.

"I'm just happy to help out the team I grew up on," Trevor said at the ice cream social opening the season. During practice he stomped around with his stopwatch and clipboard, watching our strokes and taking notes. When we were in the water, he was all business. When practice was over, he was more like a camp counselor, teaching us water-fight techniques, like how to disable your opponent with a thin, hard splash to the eyes.

"You're lucky," said Lark. "I wish he coached the diving team. I can't stand Mary-Kate."

"She's way too serious," I agreed. "She already has worry lines in her forehead."

Mary-Kate ran her team like a school of monks. While Trevor yelled at us until he was hoarse, she had the divers sit in a circle and practice visualization techniques. She walked slowly around the perimeter, saying, "Imagine yourself in perfect pike position. How does it feel in your arms? In your legs? In your shoulders? How does it feel to release the position at the end of one and a half flips?"

The fireflies were out when Lark and I walked home. They hovered above tall grasses and under dogwood trees, pulsing with light. We cupped our hands around them, careful not to touch their abdomens so they wouldn't die.

Trevor noticed Lark right away. When swim practice was over, he hung around watching the divers, but it was obvious he had his eye on her. When she wasn't up, he chatted with the swimmers crowded around him. He shushed them when it was Lark's turn.

Trevor was there the day she nailed her hardest dive. She paused at the very end of the board, her heels over the water, back to the pool, staring past the fence and the woods. Seconds later, she swooped her arms up and threw herself forward into a one and a half flip. Her body fell into the water like a knife.

Trevor whooped. "Now there's a future Division One athlete," he called out.

Mary-Kate scowled at him. She didn't believe in feedback until the end of practice. But Trevor didn't care. He clapped and cheered for Lark when she bobbed out of the water.

"He's so much nicer than Mary-Kate," she complained in a whisper. She was out of the water between dives, stuffing strands of hair under her cap.

"Trevor's the best," I agreed, although I didn't mean it. I was beginning to notice how he stirred up the energy in a group, keeping us laughing and guessing about what he would say next. Alyssa was one of his favorites because she laughed at his jokes or came back fast with one of her own. I was too shy, too slow with words to do either. Plus, I was only an average member of the team. I couldn't win his respect as an athlete. I wasn't talented like Alyssa. He lowered his voice when he talked to her and was always correcting her on her arms. With me, he was pleasant and vague. My times were good enough to get some cheery encouragement, but not much else.

I didn't really care. I loved swimming. I liked the underwater sounds and the shattered light in the blue water. It was the summer between sixth grade and seventh, and my breasts had grown overnight. I stopped taking dance class because I couldn't stand how they bounced. Swimming was the only sport where they didn't get in my way. Still, I didn't always notice when they fell out the side of my suit. "Put your girls in," Lark whispered as she passed by. She turned back to smile as she skipped off to the diving boards. She was a year older than me, but still straight up and down, muscled and fast, like a boy.

At home in my house or in my backyard, I walked around practicing my stroke, pulling the air with my arms, imagining it was water. I could feel myself getting stronger by thinking about my stroke. There was something to Mary-Kate's meditation techniques. In some ways she was a better coach than Trevor.

But then, something confusing happened, something like being erased. I got better, only Trevor didn't say anything. I saw him look at me from the corner of his eye. I felt his eyes on me when I turned away, and I was sure he was about to say something like "Good job, Mackenzie." But he never did. He moved me to the starter position on the 100-meter relay, but he didn't tell me why, and then he started yelling at me more in practice, like I was one of the lazy kids who didn't put in enough effort.

In our meet against Donaldson Run, I set out a huge lead in the relay that secured our win. I won my heat in the 25-meter butterfly. I climbed out of the pool and saw Trevor walking toward me with a huge smile on his face. He grabbed me around the shoulder and ran his knuckles over my head, his standard way of congratulating us.

That's when it happened.

"Way to go, Mackenzie!" he said, squeezing me tightly with one arm. His hand started out between my ribs and my arm. Then it slipped under my suit and cupped the curve of my breast. At first I didn't know what was happening. I thought his stopwatch must be digging into me, but it lasted too long. Then it started feeling more like what it was. I stiffened my upper arm against him to push him away, and his hand eased out. Then he was off to congratulate the other swimmers.

We won the meet. Everyone was cheering up the hill to the clubhouse, but I didn't join in. I dove back into the pool, swimming underwater, skimming the bottom until I burst through the surface gasping for air. The lifeguards were gone. I shouldn't have been in the water, but I didn't care. Trevor stood outside the locker rooms, joking with his fans, flicking a wet towel so it cracked like a whip. Laughter ricocheted off the clubhouse walls to the tennis courts. Girls ran in and out of the locker room, daring him to snap the towel. I watched, wondering if I was being overly sensitive. Maybe I was wrong. Maybe for a split second he thought I was his girlfriend. Maybe he didn't mean it and I was taking it too seriously.

I stopped swimming well. After a shower, I'd stare at myself in the mirror, disgusted with what I saw. I was so round for my age. The tops of my thighs were soft, no muscle tone at all. I would never look sleek or athletic like Lark unless I made staying thin and in shape my entire life. I was way too young to look like this.

The progress I had made evaporated. In the middle of a flip turn, I'd say to myself, *You'll never be any good. Not really. Why don't you just quit?*

"What's the matter with you, Eve?" yelled Coach Landis. "Trevor, work on her arms. Her legs are fine. It's her arms."

Trevor made me get out of the pool and show him my stroke like he did with the younger kids. I got nervous and couldn't coordinate when to rotate for a breath. He made me do it again and again like I was a beginner. Then kids popped out of the water to watch. One even jumped out to practice alongside me, and Trevor complimented him for taking the opportunity to review the basics. Undistracted, the divers practiced. Out of the corner of my eye, I saw Lark set herself up for her inward one and a half. I wanted so badly to disappear.

"Okay, Mackenzie," he said, giving me a pinch on

the outside of my arm. "Get back in the water." He turned to watch Lark.

I wanted to leave. I didn't want to get back in the pool. But leaving in front of everyone seemed even worse. I jumped back in, and the water erased me.

Finally practice was over. Kids jumped out of the water and grabbed their towels. Boys took off their caps and shook their hair. The divers gathered around Mary-Kate for final comments and notes. Kids seemed especially giddy. Laughter floated through the club. Some of the boys ran to the diving boards to show off their jackknives.

I lingered in a far corner of the pool, swimming along the bottom. I pulled at the water with all of my strength, kicking my legs until my thighs ached, wondering if this was what I had to do every moment of practice to finally get strong.

"Come on," said Lark, annoyed I wasn't out of the water yet.

"Oh, yeah . . . ," I started to lie. "I forgot to tell you. My mom's picking me up. She's gotta take me somewhere."

"Where?" she asked.

"For a fitting. I'm getting a dress made. I'm in a wedding."

"Whose?"

"My cousin's. The one in South Carolina."

"Oh," said Lark, then she scampered upstairs to the changing rooms.

I pushed off from the side of the pool, swimming underwater as far as I could without taking a breath. I burst through in the deep end, gasping for air. Up the hill, kids called out good-byes and piled into cars. The trees surrounding the club were full of dark green leaves. The sprinklers came on and showered the lawn between the pool and the parking lot. When I was sure everyone was gone, I got out.

In the dressing room, I peeled off my suit and

kicked it out of the way, hating it for being so ugly—
the stupid rainbow lettering and the leaping dolphin.
All I wanted to do was put on some dry clothes and
get home as fast as I could. I patted myself dry,
twisted the towel around my hair. That's when Trevor
came in.

"Hey," he said. He leaned against the lockers
looking at me as if I wasn't standing there naked, as if
he had run into me at the line at the snack bar.

My stomach sank and my heart started to pound.
I grabbed my towel to cover myself. "What are you
doing?"

"Oh, god! Sorry!" he laughed, pretending to be
startled. He stepped back outside but kept talking to
me through the open door. "Hope I wasn't too harsh
on you out there. You know I'm only tough on the
people I love. You okay, Eve? Wanna talk?"

His voice slid across the room, cheerful and
menacing. I pulled on my clothes and jumped on the

bench, reaching across the top of the lockers to the long, narrow louvered window. If I had to get out that way, I'd need a broom or a pole. I didn't see one. The only way out was the dressing-room door.

Someone called out to Trevor, asking him how his dad was and if his brother had given up poker and found a real job instead of cheating old guys like him out of their money. A set of keys jingled, and I edged out the door. Trevor and an old guy freckled with age spots threw back their heads and laughed at the sky. I could feel Trevor try to catch my eye, but his glance rolled off me and broke into a hundred pieces while I ran home.

Days later I was spending the night with Lark. We were making sugar cookies, decorating them with colored icing and sprinkles, eating them warm, and washing them down with milk.

"So, you really like Trevor?" I asked.

"As a guy?" She looked horrified.

"No, of course not. As a coach."

"Absolutely," she said. "I think he's awesome. He told me I could win a diving scholarship to UVA. He says I've got to carry on the Dolphin legacy. Only I don't like diving that much."

"Why not?" I asked. "You're so good at it."

"It's too . . . stunted! I mean, you take three steps, jump, flip, and then it's over. I like to cover more ground."

We went on rolling dough and cutting it into shapes. My stomach began to knot up and feel cold.

"I think he might like me . . . ," I said.

"What?" she exclaimed. She held the tube of pink icing in midair. "You're crazy."

I wanted to tell her how he touched me, how he came into the changing room when I was there, but it was obvious he had never done anything like that to her. I tried again.

"I feel him looking at me sometimes. . . ."

"It's your boobs," she said. "Guys can't help it. You should get used to it."

Finally I told my mother, but she asked the wrong questions.

"Did he touch you between your legs?"

"No."

"Were his clothes on?"

"Yes."

She leaned back and looked at me for a moment.

"Were there other people there?"

"YES!" I yelled. "I told you! The first time was at the meet. Right after my race. Everyone was there. But no one was looking at us, and even if they were, they couldn't have seen it. And the second time I was alone in the changing room."

"Tell me again; what did he do in the changing room?"

"Nothing! He looked at me! I was in there alone, and he walked in on me. He did it on purpose, and he scared me."

I started crying and my mom asked me if I wanted her to do anything, like tell Coach Landis, or take me to a therapist, and I said no. All I wanted to do was quit the team, and she said I could. So I dropped out.

I didn't know how to tell Lark that I wouldn't be going to practice anymore. At first I said I was sick and that the doctor thought I had mono. Then I said that swim team was taking too much time and that what I was really into was art. We were downstairs in her den, the darkest, coolest room in her house. The bookshelves were filled with yellowed paperbacks and old board games. We were looking for something good to watch on TV.

"But art doesn't take a lot of time," she said like I was ridiculous.

"It does if you want to be good." I passed her a magazine, pointing at a model with choppy bangs. Lark wanted a haircut.

"Okay, maybe," she said while studying the photo. "But it's not like you have to go to a separate place or do it at only certain times of the day. You can draw before practice, or when you get home. You can draw while you watch TV."

"Not if you're serious."

"But, Eve," she said, "you're not the serious type."

I flinched. It was like being slapped.

"C'mon," she pleaded. "Don't quit. Who am I gonna hang out with? Who's gonna walk with me to practice?"

By this time I was standing up. I threw the magazine to the floor. "Get your parents to drive you. They drive you everywhere else."

I stomped home, my mind flooding with all the times she broke our plans, how we always had to spend the night at her house, how she chose everything we did, whether it was beading or cutting up gossip magazines or baking cookies. I slammed my front door so hard, the pictures bounced against the wall. Then I opened the door and slammed it again. The pictures bounced and settled even more crookedly. *Good*, I thought. Every time I saw them, I'd remember how selfish Lark was. I wasn't going to be her fan anymore.

Funny. The lie I made up about drawing became a self-fulfilling prophecy. The next week my mom signed me up at the Corcoran College of Art and Design. I took classes in art history, sculpture, painting, and drawing. A curator from the museum gave a lecture on Vincent van Gogh. He projected details of his letters to his brother Theo—flowers, windmills, portraits, and night skies; sketches of windmills and canals; the bare trees and fields he saw on his long walks through the country.

At home on the shelf where my parents kept the art books, I found a collection of his letters and a huge book of all his drawings and paintings. I copied a woman sewing by a window in a straight-back chair. I drew his stark, brittle trees, rays of light, the garden of the hospital where he went to recover from fits of epilepsy and nerves.

It was like Van Gogh's feelings became mine. I stopped feeling my own because of Trevor, so I felt his instead. I read all his letters and copied out passages I liked on one wall of my room. "I want to get to a stage where it is said of my work," he wrote Theo, "this man feels deeply." I moved my grandmother's dresser so no one can read them but me.

15. Lark

I was found and buried in a stupid white dress. The woods thawed and filled again with snow. I'm transparent and pale. The dress falls to my ankles and gets in my way. The dead girls blink against the wind. I scrape away the snow to look into their faces.

I don't want to be like you, I cry.

It gets worse, says one. *Some will say it's your fault.*

For getting in the car. Or being alone. Or wearing a leotard that was cut too low in the back.

Clouds tear apart. The narrow stream gurgles in the distance, strangled by reeds and rotting leaves. Everything is silver and blank like the back of a mirror. The girls' arms are forced above their heads, strained into branches in terrible positions.

I hate this dress, I say, plucking at the hem.

You'll hate being a tree more, says the one who almost got away. I can tell by the shape of her branches. It's like she's running in air.

They say I have to find someone who will look at me, someone who is willing to see what happened to me.

Someone who loves you, says one. *Someone brave enough to learn what happened.*

Then you'll be free, says the youngest. *Not trapped like us.*

My parents? I ask.

You can try, says the one who kept watch. *They're usually not up to it.*

But I try anyway, and when I leave the woods for the first time since I'm transparent and flat, I slide between atoms. Electric charges dance on my skin and let me pass.

Porch lights glow a weary amber. Dead leaves and grasses are tipped in ice. I edge between a crack in the bricks into my house. My parents don't see me in the hall. They don't sense me following them into separate rooms—my father in the study, my mother in my bedroom. She opens drawers and runs her hands over my clothes. She pulls strands of hair from my brush, buries her face deep in my pillows trying to catch my scent. She can't pick up the clothes I left scattered or wipe away the stain from my last cup of tea. She sleeps on the floor in my room, twisted in blankets, dreaming about finding me before I die. Her own room is silent. Clothes hang in her closet.

Her shoes are perfectly arranged.

At his desk, my father searches the internet for support groups for parents of murdered children. He thinks my mother is the one who needs it most. The computer casts his face in blue light. His posture, as always, is perfect. Nearby are sharp pencils and a pad of yellow paper. He needs duties and goals to list and cross off. I lay my hand on his shoulder and breathe close to his ear, but my breath is an absence, empty as a zero, a spot of nothing in the air.

Dejected, I tell the girls they were right.

Think of someone else, says another. *A friend, not a relative.*

My mind sorts through faces and names. I didn't realize how lonely I was in my life. My last true friend was Eve, but then we had a fight and never made up. The girls at gymnastics pretended to be my friends, but I knew they were happy when I injured my knee. At school I maximized my time, working on homework during free periods and at lunch instead of hanging out with friends. I stopped going to games and plays. I quit working on the newspaper.

Think! says the youngest. *Or else you'll be like us. Who was the last person you enjoyed spending time with? Who was the last person who made you laugh?*

Nyetta, I say.

16. *Nyetta*

Hallie lets her sons watch TV
and play video games. They eat processed sugar and
drink nonorganic milk. My mom's afraid I'll be cor-
rupted. She hates it when I go over to that house. My
dad's waiting for me in the driveway. He doesn't like
to come in because he says my mom always starts a
fight.

"Call me if you want to come home early," says

my mom. She opens the door and watches me leave.

"Hey, you," says my dad with a smile. He backs out the driveway and heads to the parkway. He's in a big hurry. "The boys can't wait to see you. They've challenged us to a Ping-Pong tournament."

I sincerely doubt this, but I don't say anything.

Hallie's house is a big white farmhouse near Chain Bridge. It's one of the oldest houses around, with an attic and a root cellar and a little closet in the kitchen called a larder that's for things like onions and carrots. Everything is dirty in the right way, like a sprinkle of crumbs on the cutting board and flowers spilling petals from a vase on the windowsill.

She doesn't mind if you spill your juice because she only has things that can't be ruined.

"After all, I have boys," she says, "and a hairy old dog."

My mom's house is totally different. We have lots of special things. Most of them are very old.

Antiquities, to be exact. My mom started collecting them before I was born. We have mummy beads and urns, coins, oil lamps, a tiny alabaster Venus, and three pomegranates carved from stone. Each one is in a little case because they are so delicate and rare that even the dust shouldn't touch them.

Downstairs in the basement, the boys, my father, and I are having the tournament. The boys slam the ball back and forth. They know how to use topspin and make tricky shots. Zeke dashes to the side of the table and taps the ball just over the net so it's impossible to return. He almost has dreadlocks. Anders's hair is straight. My dad and I are ahead because he makes the most shots.

Dad bought them the Ping-Pong table and turned the basement into his office. He has a tiny desk for his computer, a two-drawer file cabinet, and a few shelves of books. He used to work all the time when he lived with us. He stacked books in every room—on the dining table, the floor near his bed, the kitchen counter, and the coffee table. He took a laptop to bed every night. When he moved in with Hallie, he stopped stacking books and gave up his laptop.

Anders serves me an easy shot, which I return, but of course I miss the next, and the next, and the next. I can't do anything with a ball, no matter what size it is. The boys pull ahead, and my dad starts missing shots, on purpose, I think. I stop even trying. Anders and Zeke lose interest. They turn on the PlayStation and huddle over the controls. I guess the tournament is over.

"Can we do something else?" I ask.

Upstairs in the kitchen, Hallie is making bread. She gives me an apron and shows me how to dust the top of the dough with flour so it doesn't stick when you knead it. There's always a project when I come over, like baking, or making jewelry, or sewing tote bags out of old fabric she bought at a flea market. She set up her loom in the guest bedroom, the room where I sleep, and she's promised to teach me how to weave a blanket.

"That's good," she says as I fold the dough over on itself. She has Zeke's curly hair—tight blond ringlets that start at her scalp and loosen at the ends. She's wearing white yoga pants and a white long-sleeve T-shirt. A tiny gold Buddha dangles from a cord around her neck. A bracelet of rose quartz wraps around her wrist. Lark would say she's too limber from all that yoga.

"You better strengthen your core," I tell her.

"Think so?" she asks.

Then she jumps into a whole new topic.

"Your dad says you're still home from school."

I start kneading with more enthusiasm. I sprinkle flour and fold and push and fold. If I do everything right, Hallie might drop the subject.

She greases two bowls with a stick of butter. "He says you talk to the girl who died."

I throw the dough on the breadboard and slap it a few times.

"Her name was Lark, right?"

I toss the dough from one hand to the other. It's smooth and elastic, and I can smell the yeast.

"I talk to my therapist about Lark," I tell her.

"Good," says Hallie. "It must be awful to know someone who died in such a terrible way."

"I try not to think about it," I lie.

I watch her divide and smooth the dough into two halves. She puts each one in a buttered bowl and covers them with tea towels.

"Now what?" I ask.

"Now we wait. You'll see. They'll double in size."

I lift the towels for one last look. It's hard to believe the dough will rise to the towel, but two hours later it has. And then we punch it down and knead it some more, and then it rises again, and then we bake it. I can't wait for it to cool, so Hallie lets me cut one loaf even though you shouldn't cut warm bread. The butter melts as soon as I spread it. It runs between my fingers as I take my first bite. The taste is full and rich, a little salty sweet. It's like I am eating a world of cottages and water mills, wildflowers and deer that come out of the forest to eat from my hand. Hallie watches me and smiles, and for a moment I almost forget where I am.

17. *Eve*

It's almost seven fifteen, and I'm rushing through breakfast. My parents have been up for hours, as usual, working in their studios. They're taking a coffee break, but also hanging out in the kitchen to check in with me before I go to school. It's their new habit—checking my vitals from a distance. My mom creeps around and stares, then throws in little conversation openers, like

"The kids at school must be really upset." (Not really.)

Or

"Do you ever get frightened because of what happened to Lark?" (Yes.)

Or

"This must be very sad for you." (It is.)

"I talked with Lark's parents last night," says Dad. He's sitting at the breakfast table with the paper spread out in front of him. My mother sips her coffee. Her apron is stained with clay fingerprints. "They've put the house on the market."

"Are you kidding?" I ask.

"Seems like a good idea," says my mom.

"Maybe no one will buy it," I say. "Who would want to buy the house where a dead girl lived?"

"We live in a very good neighborhood," says my father. "Even in this economy, I think it will sell quickly."

"I hope not," I say. "I hope they decide to board it up for a while, then move back." I can imagine all the furniture covered in white sheets and the shutters closed.

My mom has something to say, but she's unsure about how to bring it up. I can feel her trying to take my pulse from her vantage point at the stove. I hurriedly scoop up the last bits of cereal at the bottom of the bowl, hoping she'll think I'm in too much of a rush to bother. It doesn't work.

"Eve, have you thought about taking that women's self-defense class?"

"No."

"I think it would be good for you."

"I think it would freak me out more."

She starts to say how the class might "empower" me, but I shush her before she gets it out.

Last night it dropped below freezing. The last bits of snow froze over again. Tiny icebergs at the corners of driveways glint in the sun. Up ahead, some boys are packing them into hard snowballs and throwing them full force at one another. They'd sting like hell if they hit the neck or the face, but the boys don't care. They're aiming and throwing, running and dodging like they're playing war. One of them isn't wearing gloves, and his hands are pink with cold. He laughs and takes aim at his friend, who crouches behind a car. The wind has picked up. I tuck in my chin and brace against it.

Throughout the day, my mind wanders between Lark's house and my new book on Van Gogh. I don't think about how Lark died anymore, more about little things, like what it's going to be like to see a For Sale sign in her front yard and then how weird it will be if another family actually moves in. Mr. Haus goes on and on about the Persian wars and why the Greeks finally won. I'm copying his notes from the chalkboard and trying to finish the sketch of the fountain in the courtyard of Van Gogh's asylum at the same time. Poor guy. He wore himself out looking for God and arguing with Gauguin. I'm drawing from memory, trying to capture the ellipse of the fountain and the sharp angles of the trees. My right hand is flying. My left is holding up my glasses so they don't fall into my notebook. The bell rings, but I don't move. My drawing is almost finished.

"Eve," Mr. Haus says softly. "You're going to be late."

In Debate, Ms. Curren has mercifully decided it's our group's turn to research in the library. Scott and Darren give each other high fives. Judith takes the pass for the four of us, and off we trot. The boys take a side trip to shoot some hoops, while Judith and I dutifully hit the books.

"Look for a quote from some expert or official," Judith orders, passionless. "I'll get some statistics about the high cost of research."

Between the two of us, we could finish all the research we need in about three hours. Darren and Scott are mostly a hindrance. We don't even bother to think of something for them to do.

I type in "opposition to stem cell research" and am flooded with hits. Senators, ministers, scientists, and right-to-life advocates all have something to say. There's massive concern for the unborn. I scroll down until I find the speech of a molecular biologist who reminds us that Congress declared life begins at conception. Therefore, harvesting stem cells is tantamount to murder. It's irritating to take notes on why the government shouldn't help scientists find cures for diabetes and multiple sclerosis, but I'm happy to be here and not in the classroom. My pen glides across paper.

Behind me there's a rustle of backpacks and chimes from a cell phone. A mob of juniors pulls in. They descend on the computers, and the guy sitting down on my right is Ian, the writer for the paper, the guy whose eyes met mine at the end of the pep rally.

"Hey," he says.

"Hey," I say back.

"You knew Lark Austin, right?"

My face gets warm. My answer is muffled, like I'm speaking through a scarf. "Yes."

"I did, too."

"How?" I ask. His eyes are the blue in *Starry Night*, expansive and cobalt, surrounded by black lashes. My heart stirs a little, like it's swimming inside me. If I ever wanted to draw him, I'd have to use colored ink—maybe Bombay blue.

"Lark took journalism last year."

"She gave it up for gymnastics," I say.

"Yeah, I remember. Too bad. She was a good writer. I drove her home once. I think I saw you. You live next door, right?"

He reaches over the keyboard to shake my hand.

"I'm Ian."

"I'm Eve."

His hand touches mine. There are muscles where the fingers meet the palm, and the hollow is deep, like it could cup water.

"How are her parents?" he asks.

"Not very good. They want to move."

"I don't blame them," he said.

He logs on while I print out the speech of the molecular biologist. Scott and Darren tumble by to see if there's anything to do. They're red faced from shooting hoops in the cold. Their hats are on backward. All they need are little propellers and they could be Tweedledee and Tweedledum. They're making a ruckus, dropping books and dissing each other. The librarian threatens to send them back to class. I get the speech from the printer and hand it to them.

"Read this," I say. "Look for a quote we can use

in our opening remarks."

When I get back to the computer, Ian is looking at my sketchbook.

"Hey!" I say, grabbing it back.

"Sorry," he says, "but you left it open. I didn't touch it. You're so good!"

"No," I say. The sharp corner stabs the pad of my thumb.

"Yes! I like that old lady, and the windmill along the canal. Have you been to the Netherlands?"

"No," I say, "but I'd like to. . . . I'm into Van Gogh. I'm studying his art. I copy a lot of his drawings."

"That's cool. I thought Van Gogh was famous for his paintings."

"He is, but I like his drawings better."

"That's cool," he said. "There are lots of great abandoned buildings in the Netherlands. You into that—ruined buildings taken over by nature?"

"Sounds interesting."

"It is," he says. He's focused and lit up, like all sorts of ideas are firing inside his brain. "I know a bunch of cool websites to check out."

I'm dying to hear more, but his friend calls out from the magazine rack. "Hey, Ian," he says. "Here's that interview you were talking about."

"Gotta go," he tells me. "Talk to you later."

He bounds over to his crowd of juniors, not bothering to log off the computer.

Days later, he's in the hall with the other journalism students passing out the new issue of the paper. He points to the story about Lark on the front page. There's a photo of a grief counselor talking to a class, and another one of students huddling at a table in the library drawing pictures and writing poems.

"Why isn't there a picture of Lark?" I ask.

"Look at the back."

The entire back page is a blowup of Lark's school portrait. Underneath, in wispy font, it says,

Lark Austin

Forever in our hearts

Finally, you can fly. . . .

"It's disgusting," I say.

"I know."

"What's that supposed to mean, 'Finally, you can fly'?"

"It's supposed to 'honor her love for gymnastics,' says the senior editor."

"Well, it's disgusting."

He shrugs and sighs. "I agree."

I keep staring at the photo and hating it. Ian takes a step back.

"Well," he says, "I gotta go. I wanted to make sure you saw it."

He's wearing a huge striped sweater that's unraveling at the sleeves. He'd look lost in it, but his shoulders and back are all muscle because he's on crew.

"Thanks," I say. "I know it's not your fault."

"Hey," he says. "This Friday I'm hearing a band you might like. Would you like to come?"

The concert is in an old movie theater that Ian says was built in the twenties when films were still silent and vaudeville acts used to perform on the stage. He takes a picture of me in the lobby between sconces shaped like candles; only the flame-shaped bulbs are burned out. Ian says he's never seen them lit up. The walls are covered in painted fabric that's been fading and unraveling for almost a hundred years.

"The owner is trying to sell," says Ian, shaking his head. "Can you imagine what a tragedy it would be if someone knocked it down?"

Ian points to the huge chandelier in the lobby. Strings of crystals and beads drape from a recessed painting of peacocks and classical ruins.

"You could draw that," he says encouragingly.

"You're good enough to draw this whole place."

His hand is warm and smooth. I imagine the theater being taken over by trees. Saplings break through the floors. Vines suffocate the walls, pulling them into the earth.

All the seats on the first floor have been torn up so people can stand by the stage or dance. Ian leads me to the balcony so we can sit down and talk. The seats are the old-fashioned kind with inlaid brass numbers and velvet cushions. We sit in the front row, dangling our hands over the railing, looking down at the crowd that's already pushed against the stage.

"Don't hate me," I say, "but my dad builds McMansions."

"Oh, no," he groans, rubbing my hands like I'm cold. "You poor girl."

The DJ plays Brian Eno and Stone Roses and Joy Division, which Ian says are good choices since they've all influenced Sky Crush, the band we're about to hear.

The opening act is a band from Portland called the Substitutes that projects educational filmstrips from the Cold War about personal hygiene, the growing threat of communism, and how to respond in case of nuclear attack. The songs are short and angry, with driving beats overlaying thrashing guitars. I put my hands over my ears, but the music is still so loud I can feel my bones vibrate. On the screen, primary-school kids are ducking under their desks. A map of the Soviet Union turns into an evil octopus spreading its tentacles over Europe and Asia. A high school girl points to a pimple on her chin and frowns.

At intermission we go downstairs to the little bar that used to be a hatcheck booth when people wore hats and gloves. Ian buys us each a Coke, then leads me outside to a patio where people go to smoke and get some fresh air. A woman with a boy's haircut and silver hair lifts up her throat to laugh. Her date smiles at her with glittering wolf teeth.

Ian pulls out a tiny bottle of rum from his coat pocket, the kind you buy on airplanes.

"Want some?" he offers.

"Sure," I say, and he pours some into my drink. "What about you?"

"I'm driving," he says, shaking his head. "Gotta get you home safe. I promised your dad."

I take a long sip of my drink. Rum clings to the ice cubes and makes me shudder. People around us laugh and talk. Their cigarettes glow and send out curls of white smoke. Above us a square of sky is speckled with stars. Ian pours the rest of the rum over the ice cubes, and a few sips later I'm instantly relaxed, as if I've let two heavy packages fall to the floor.

We drift back to the balcony. Other couples mill around us. Going down the stairs, I stumble a little. I'm not used to drinking, so I lean slightly into him and he puts his arm around me until we get to our seats. Onstage the roadies unwind cables and set up the mikes. Finally, the lights go down, and Sky Crush takes the stage. It's a band of two, a girl and a guy, both skinny and tall with pale oval faces. They could be brother and sister, but Ian says they grew up together in a beach town in Delaware. In high school they started recording waves crashing and boardwalk sounds like the *whoosh* of the roller coaster, the calliope of the merry-go-round, and a wooden ball rolling up the skee-ball ramp in the arcade. He says they have a whole library of sounds that they edit and splice and include in their songs. The girl looks like she stepped out of a Pre-Raphaelite painting. Her long auburn hair falls over her face as she sings and plays keyboards. Sometimes it sounds like an organ, sometimes a harpsichord. The guy plays gamelan and slide guitar, adding layers of sounds from a laptop hooked up to a tiny speaker. Between the vocals I hear distant laughter and bells, and the three-four rhythm of a ragged waltz played by old men in a plaza. The girl's voice floats above the texture of sounds, coaxing you to listen like the waves in a shell. It makes me think of Van Gogh walking in the fog sketching windmills and geese, his red beard and blue eyes the only bright colors in an expanse of gray.

After the final song, the curtain falls, and the dusty chandeliers flicker awake. People put on their coats and leave their drinks on the floor. Outside it's windy and cold, and the music still clings to me like a dream.

"Did you like it?" asks Ian.

"Yeah," I say. "I'm still dreaming."

Ian laughs. "I knew you were the one to take to Sky Crush."

"Why?"

"Because," he replies, "you're an artist. Like they are."

"I don't know what that means," I say, confused.

"I think it means you see things, hear things, that most people miss."

I'm embarrassed and pleased, then suddenly disappointed. "So, would you take a different girl to a different concert?"

"What do you mean?" he asks.

"I mean, is this what you do? Match a girl to a band, then ask her out when it comes to town?"

"No . . . ," he says tentatively.

"Because if it is," I sputter, "if this is what you do . . ."

"No," he insists. "It isn't what I do. I didn't want to take anyone else to a concert. I wanted to take you."

"Why?" I ask, but he doesn't answer. Instead he pulls the belt of my coat so I fall into him, then he presses his lips against mine.

"Stop it," I say, pushing him away.

He looks embarrassed and a little shocked. "I'm sorry," he says. "I . . . I thought . . ."

"Wait," I say. "Wait . . ."

I stand apart, thinking of Trevor and the strange mix of feelings I used to have around him. Feelings of being excited and dismissed, invited, then ignored. I didn't want Trevor to touch me or see me. I didn't want him to put his hand on me or sneak up on me when I was naked.

But Ian, I tell myself, *is nothing like Trevor.* His eyes search mine, and I feel myself reaching up to him from the bottom of a well.

"Yes," I say, "I do want you to kiss me."

And he does, and the boundaries between us start to blur. I can feel his heart against mine, beating under our sweaters and coats while the wind swirls the night stars.

18. *Lark*

It was past midnight, and the poor girl was still awake, sitting on the floor clutching a pillow, her ear to the wall. Her mom was on the phone, yelling at her dad, screaming that he's ruined her life, and isn't it great that he gets to start over with a new house and a new wife, and a new family. Even I was frightened by the bitterness in her voice.

I inched closer and put my hand on Nyetta's

shoulder. She turned around and shivered.

"You're pale," she said.

"I'm dead."

"I know."

Nyetta turned back to the wall. "My mom is so sad. I don't know what to do."

"Listen," I say, "I need a favor."

19. *Nyetta*

April has given up asking about Lark. Now she wants to know all about the divorce and how it affected me, and if my parents used to fight. I tell her not really, which is the truth because I've decided not to lie about my family life. Only about my ghost life.

"But for a while my mother went crazy," I say, then I go on to tell her how once my mom woke me up in the middle of the night and drove me to Hallie's house to tell my dad to come home because the divorce wasn't final. It was cold and she forgot my robe, and I was shivering when I rang the bell and waited on the step. My mother sat in the car with the motor running. I could see the silhouettes of my father and a woman sitting at a table through the window. I didn't know Hallie then. She didn't invite me inside. Instead she called my dad to the door, and he told me to tell my mom to take me home.

"Get some sleep," he said. "I'll call you tomorrow."

So my mom drove home, then she sent me to bed, but I didn't go to sleep. Instead I took out all my dolls from the closet and set them up like groups of sisters and mothers, aunts and daughters, in kitchens and schools and living rooms where they would read books and draw pictures or teach one another the alphabet or how to play an instrument. My entire room became their dollhouse. They slept under the armchair because that's where it was dark. My desk was the music room and the second-floor study. The shoe boxes in the closet were kitchen counters. I drew knobs and rings on one to be the stove.

April puts down her pencil. "What your mother did was very unfair to you. You didn't want to go to Hallie's house at night. She did. And then she made you be the one to ask him to come home."

"But I didn't," I said. "I couldn't. I just stood there on the porch."

"Do you feel guilty about not doing what your mother asked?"

"Kind of."

"What she asked you to do was inappropriate. Adults shouldn't tell their children to do things they can't or won't do for themselves."

Why not? I wonder. It seems to me parents do this all the time. They want their children to make them happy and proud. Lark's parents wanted her to get a gymnastics scholarship to college because it was the next best thing to being in the Olympics. I could tell she felt sad she wasn't good enough for that.

April interrupts me.

"Next time your mother or father, or any adult, asks you to do something that's inappropriate, you can say no."

Her advice floats by. I think about how serious Lark was. I wonder if it made her happy or sad to be like that. On the outside, she was happy, but some people keep things to themselves. Sometimes her knee hurt so bad, she limped.

April watches me the way you watch the weather change in the sky. "It can be difficult to learn how to say no," she says. "We can practice next week."

At night Lark decides to drop by for one of her visits. She's dirty, like someone who's been spending too much time outdoors. She's not asking me to look at her wound anymore. Mostly she wants me to see how she's turning into a tree. It's sort of a guilt trip.

Little buds of leaves are growing between her fingers, and her hair is wild and full. She lowers her head, and I can see tiny strands of ivy growing out of her scalp.

"My heart is wood now," she says mournfully.

"That doesn't happen."

"It has to me."

"No," I say. "You still have feelings."

"Not really."

"Then why are you here?"

She sighs. Tears cut through the dirt on her face. "You're right," she says. "I hate being dead."

Poor Lark. She loved having a body. It was her favorite part of being alive. "I'll try harder," I tell her.

Lark brightens, then she starts to lift her dress, but I turn away.

"Look at me!" she yells, pulling at her hair and pushing up her sleeves. Her arms are rough and brown. "It's happening! Right now!"

The door to my mother's office creaks open. Her footsteps pound down the hallway.

"My mother's coming," I whisper.

Lark scowls back. "She can't hear me."

"Be quiet!" I whisper.

"I won't! What's the big deal about a stab wound? Don't you realize what's happening to me? Don't you know that the only thing worse than what that man did to me is turning into a tree? You're not worried about your mother. You're putting me off because you're a coward."

"Stop!" I say.

"And you're selfish! So what if you have a few more nightmares? I'm about to lose my body forever! I'm about to turn into a tree!"

But it's too awful to see, too terrible to see the cut in her side, the place where the knife went in. I can't do it without fainting or getting sick or so scared that

I might never come back from being afraid.

"I can't," I say. "I will later. I promise. I want to help, but I can't right now."

Lark shakes her head. "Forget it. You had your chance. I'm never coming back here. I'm going to find someone else."

Outside the wind picks up. It thrashes the trees and shrieks through the neighborhood. Shingles lift off roofs and gates clatter. Lark opens my window and slips out, legs first.

"Good-bye."

The curtains billow and snap in a riot of anger and frost. A gust of cold wind blows into my face. When I open my eyes, she's gone.

"Lark!" I lean out the window, calling after her. "Come back!"

The clouds break and a sleeting rain falls. I'm pelted in the face, and my wet nightgown sticks to my skin. The rain is so cold, it stings. I leap to the ground and run through the gate at the edge of my yard. Broken branches pull out the hem of my nightgown. Fir trees rattle their dry cones. I fall and pick myself up and run into the woods. Eyes flash in the dark, eyes of dead girls caught in trees.

"Little Night! Little Night!" they sing bitterly, mocking my name, hating me for failing Lark. "You're too late. She's like us now!"

The rain turns to ice. The sky collapses in snow. I cross the creek, cracking paper-thin ice, cutting my feet on sharp stones. Lark waits on the other side, so white she is almost blue.

"I'm here. I'm ready now," I say. And I am. I'm tired of being afraid. I don't want to be the one who fails her in the end.

I stretch out my hand. Before my eyes, her fingernails extend into thin roots that wrap around my wrist and pull me into her.

"Too late, too late, too late," she says, sounding

both mournful and pleased. I don't know what she is now. Ghost or tree? Girl or wood?

I try to draw back my hand.

"Let me go," I cry. I dig my heels into the cold earth and struggle against her.

Behind me I hear running footsteps and someone yelling. It's my mother. She pulls me away from the tree, and I fall into her arms. I hear the panic in her voice as she tries to help me stand. Finally she scoops me in her arms and carries me home. The trees shake their branches at me. They would like to tangle my hair and scratch my skin. All Lark wanted was someone to see what happened to her, but I'm only a girl, too afraid to look.

MAN ARRESTED IN
DEATH OF TEENAGER

—◄○►—

MARCH 7: A 29-year-old man faces arraignment next week after his arrest for the murder of a 16-year-old girl whose body was found in a heavily wooded area of Potomac Overlook Park. Police say they arrested Stephen Blaire before noon yesterday at his Fairfax apartment on suspicion of first-degree murder in the death of Lark Austin.

She was declared missing on January 24 after disappearing after her gymnastics lesson. She was found two days later, beaten and stabbed and dead from exposure after the area's first major snowstorm. Detectives have not yet revealed what led them to arrest Blaire.

20. *Eve*

Under my window, men carry boxes from Lark's house to a moving van parked in her driveway. They trundle out pictures and furniture wrapped in packing blankets. It makes me sick to think about someone else living there. Van Gogh wouldn't want the Austins to sell their house. And if they did, he'd draw it at least a dozen times before they left. And then again after they left. But never once after the other people moved in.

Ian is in his nerdy glasses and a red thrift-shop wool sweater. He lies on my bed while I crosshatch the shutters. I'm scribbling, building up texture, defining boundaries of stucco and wood, trying to capture what I know before the new owners completely destroy it with some ghastly remodel. I've given Ian a reading assignment—Van Gogh's letters to Theo, the ones where he writes about the colors of the soil, wheat, and sky, and how he has to buy more canvas right away so he can capture it all before the season changes.

Ian crosses an ankle over a knee. His mouth is slightly open because he's concentrating. He is completely, utterly adorable.

"I love them," he says. "But why do you? They're all about color and you don't paint. You only draw in black."

I think about the paints in my father's studio.

Paints made of pigments and oils, egg yolk and minerals. Paints from England in little lead tubes. I remember squeezing out pearls of paint. The colors were so bright, they made my eyes vibrate.

"Color's hard to manage." I can't say what scares me about the loss of clear lines, the blur of edges.

"But you love it," Ian insists, holding up the book. It's open to a detail of sunflowers against a bright yellow background. Petals spiral with brushstrokes of vermilion and orange. The stone I buried deep in my chest begins to cut its way to the surface.

My mom knocks on the door while I'm formulating a response. She carries an armload of whites.

"I'm feeling generous," she says. "I'll do yours, but only if you give them to me right now."

It's her third interruption since Ian arrived. She's brought us a tray of sandwiches and grapes. She's hovering, trying to help us make good decisions. I look through my hamper and hand her some clothes.

"By the way, " she says on her way out, "the Austins are having a little gathering for Lark's friends next week. They want her friends to choose something to remember her."

"I'm not going," I say. "I don't want anything."

"You might later," she says.

"Mom, in case you didn't notice, Lark and I weren't friends anymore. We've barely talked since middle school."

"Think of it as a gift," she says. "Something her parents are offering you and something you can give them. Simply by being there."

"You should go," says Ian.

I glare at him.

"I'll take you," he offers.

My mom beams. "Thanks, Ian," she says, and leaves without closing the door. A sock falls to the floor.

If it were another book he was reading, I'd pull it

from Ian's hands and hit him with it. But it's Volume II of my Bulfinch edition of *The Complete Letters of Vincent van Gogh*, the one with the dark blue cover and the gold cypress tree on the spine. "Give me that," I say. "Now."

He complies. I place it gently on the floor. Then I sucker punch him in the upper arm, but he's too fast for me. He flexes his biceps so it almost hurts me as much as it does him.

"OWWW!" he says.

"Traitor."

"What do you mean, traitor? That's a bit extreme."

"I don't want to go."

"It's polite," he says. "It's what you do when someone dies."

He holds me tight, and I bury my face in his neck. He smells like frost and leaves and cold air. I can feel all types of bad choices coming on. Ian throws a leg over mine, then rolls me over in some kind of ninja move so that now he's on top looking down at me. I see his rumpled black hair and white skin, his sapphire blue eyes. I keep staring, waiting, then he rolls me back over. He gets up and sits away from me, his back against the wall.

"Is something wrong?" he asks. "Are you okay when I get physical with you?"

Suddenly I'm cold. A voice inside says to say nothing, but words catch up and fight in my throat. The stone deep inside me tears through muscle and skin.

"I—I—I need to tell you something. . . ." And I do. Words stumble and fall out of me. Sounds of my mother doing the laundry float upstairs, punctuating the silence while I try to find words. I tell him about Trevor, how scared I was in the dressing room, how I tried to tell Lark, how my mom didn't do anything once I finally told her.

"It's like she didn't get it. She didn't get how it

made me feel. She was focused on other things, like if he went inside me or not, or if she had to take me to the doctor."

Ian looks at me, then away, resting his head behind clasped hands. It must be a burden to hear this.

"But I like when we're physical," I say. I'm shaking now. My breath cuts off so I can only whisper. "I do. I'm not always sure how to respond, but I like when we're physical. And I want you to like me that way."

Ian crosses the room and folds me into his arms. He kisses my hair while I lean into him. "Listen to me," he says. "That Trevor guy is an asshole. He's a child molester and a pervert. You're with me now, and nothing like that can ever happen to you again."

21. *Lark*

I'm monstrous and ugly—part tree, part girl, the color of dirt and bark. Leaves cover my face. I blend in with the woods, like a fallen tree or a stump, a branch torn off by a storm. I stand by the trees by my house, watching Ian and Eve walk from her house to mine. I hear Eve describing the games that we played in the den, how we made collages with scented markers and glitter.

"Why are you telling me this?" he asks, drawing her close.

"Because you liked her," she says. "Didn't you?"

I wait to hear what he says. I remember how I used to blush when he walked into class, how he smiled and dropped his head when he took the desk next to mine.

"Only a little," he says. "I gave up quick. She was hard to get to know. I couldn't have a conversation with her."

"Not like with me?"

"No. Not like with you."

I watch him kiss Eve, and I have never felt more dead than I do now. I remember how I liked his voice, and how his eyes always seemed to be dilated. I didn't have room for him. I cast out Eve as well because she didn't keep up with her swimming. I was all about practice and regionals, competitions and grades. The week before I died my mother signed me up for an SAT prep course. I was dead when I was alive, and I didn't even know it.

22. *Nyetta*

It's almost noon, but I'm still in bed, wrapped in my blanket. My mother paces the hall and talks to my dad on the phone, describing how she found me collapsed in the woods.

"It was snowing and she was facedown, crying and hallucinating, talking to Lark." She's crying like she doesn't know what to do. Next she's on the phone to April, telling her the same thing. When she comes into my room, I pretend I'm asleep.

I hear a car in the driveway and a knock on the door. Moments later, my dad walks into my room.

"Hey, you," he says. "How're you feeling?" I let him hold me against him and rock me like he did when I was little.

My mom comes in with a tray of soup and crackers, and a glass of apple juice mixed with sparkling water. My parents sit on my bed and watch me eat. The broth trickles down my throat. My throat feels swollen and sore. Either Lark or I broke my window because one pane is patched with brown paper and tape.

"I'll go to the hardware store later," my dad says.

"Can I come?" I ask.

"Maybe," he says.

"After you see April," says my mother.

"But it's not Wednesday," I say. I'm drowsy and thick, like there's a cloud in my head. "I don't want to go. I'm not feeling well." But my parents say I have to go. They tell me to finish my soup and get dressed.

Strangely, the three of us go in my dad's car, something that hasn't happened in years. I'm on the alert, waiting for the fighting to start. But it doesn't. Seeing the backs of their heads so close together makes me remember what it was like before the divorce. I feel like crying, but I don't.

April's cheery and welcoming, especially to my father, whom she hasn't met before. She ushers me into her office and settles into her big comfy chair. She asks me if I know why my parents wanted me to see her today, and I say it's because I was outside last night when I should have been in bed.

"Were you running away?" she asks.

"Of course not," I say.

"Your mother says you were talking to Lark."

"It was a dream," I say.

"Your parents wonder if you should live with your

dad for a while. They think a change might be good for you."

I tell April that's a stupid idea, and when she asks why, I remind her I'm homeschooled.

"Hallie isn't smart enough to teach me. My mother has a PhD."

"I don't think they imagine you staying there for an extended period of time."

"Whatever," I say.

"They think the change would do you some good. After all, you have two little stepbrothers there, and a new stepmother you've told me you like. . . ."

"I never said I like Hallie. . . ."

"Sorry," says April. "My mistake. But you have spoken well of her. She's offered to teach you how to weave, am I right?"

"She's okay," I say. "A little too namby-pamby for my taste."

April shrugs. "Maybe it would be good to spend

some time in the home of a namby-pamby woman for a while. The way you've described her makes me think she's rather . . . nurturing."

"Too nurturing! Those boys are incredibly spoiled."

"Maybe she'd spoil you. You could use some spoiling. After all, you've been through so much."

"Really?" I ask.

"Really," says round-faced April. "Your father's departure, your parents' divorce, your mother's anger, the violent death of the person you most looked up to . . . these are all very difficult experiences, very draining, exhausting events for anyone, but especially for someone your age."

It's cold in her office. I pull the pink-and-blue quilt off the ottoman and wrap it around my shoulders. It's decorated with hobbyhorses and ABC blocks.

"They're worried that you were talking to Lark last night."

"They don't have to be. Lark won't visit me anymore."

"Why not?"

"Because I let her down."

"How did you do that?"

"I wouldn't look where the knife went in. Now she'll really die. That tree where she was killed is swallowing her up."

"Oh, dear," says April. "Why would the tree do that to her?"

"Because that's what happens to girls who are killed the way Lark was. Don't you know?"

"No," says April, "but I'd like to. Will you tell me?"

"Some trees have a girl in them."

When I'm done, April sends me out to the waiting room and asks my parents inside. I sit on the floor, looking through a basket of broken toys and torn books. An assortment of Happy Meal toys, Lego key chains, and metal cars with missing tires are all tangled together in the mane of a My Little Pony. *April should do something about this*, I think. It could make kids think she doesn't really care about helping them.

23. *Eve*

Upstairs in the attic, Ian and I
sweep down the rafters and wash them with pine soap.
We paint the walls white, scrub the one tiny window,
hang a few clip lights and strings of Christmas lights
from the beams. My dad and Ian carry up a worktable
and chair and an old velvet armchair I found at the
flea market. When it's spring, my dad says, he'll put
in skylights so I'll be able to paint by natural light.

Shelves of my dad's old paints and brushes, glass jars of pigments, and all my Van Gogh books line one of the walls.

Ian sits in the chair while I take his picture.

"I hate this," he says.

"Just look at the camera," I say. "Or don't." I take a few of his profile, amazed at how long his lashes are. I look through the photos carefully, searching for the right one. I'll paint him in wild blue and orange, swirls of celadon in the back.

It's the night of the wake, and Ian walks me to Lark's door and rings the bell. A woman named Carole asks us inside. She says she's Lark's aunt. Ian kisses me good-bye, and the door closes behind him.

The foyer is shockingly bare. The table where the family left keys and letters is gone. The family photos have been taken down, leaving dark rectangles on the walls. Bolts of bubble wrap and boxes are stacked in the corner. I ask where Lark's parents are, but Carole says they decided not to stay.

"I don't think they realized how hard it would be to see all of Lark's friends. . . ." Her voice trails off. "It's too much for them right now."

In the living room, different groups of Lark's friends acknowledge one another with small glances and smiles. Nyetta, the girl down the street, sits on a love seat with her mother and father and her father's new wife. Girls from school stand around the fireplace while Lark's friends from gymnastics gather around the sofa. They wear the red-and-white ribbon from their uniform in their hair. Mothers stand around a card table in the corner of the room. They take turns arranging platters of food and serving drinks. I wish I could join them so I'd have something to do. Instead I make my way to the girls from school. Alyssa is there. I'm surprised at first, but then I remember how she knew Lark from the pool and stayed on the swim team long after I left.

"Hey," she says.

"Hi," I say back.

"This is pretty horrible, isn't it?" She lets her hair fall over her face, like a veil so we can confide. Away from Boston and Beth, she's more calm and subdued.

"Yeah," I answer.

"I hear you're going out with Ian. That must be kinda weird . . . him being the only guy Lark ever really liked."

"I didn't know Lark liked him," I lie. "I wasn't as close to her as I used to be."

"No one was. But she liked him, I could tell."

I get a little flustered and jealous, which she must have noticed, because she rushes to add that she didn't think Ian ever liked her. "Not to be mean . . . but Lark kind of disappeared from us, didn't she? I remember when you two were best friends."

Lark's aunt invites us upstairs to her room, which is still unpacked and only slightly different from the last time I was there. The bed is made, the same flowered quilt and embroidered pillows, and her desk is still covered with schoolbooks. Above it used to be pictures of pop stars and movies that she loved, but now a collage of photos from her meets is pinned to the wall. In one Lark flies over the top uneven bar in a back flip. Her gaze is focused, thighs pulled, feet pointed, hands ready to grip. I can't imagine anyone being stronger, or knowing her body in space better than Lark did, and I wonder how this could have happened to her. Why couldn't she fight him off?

Lark's aunt steps to the middle of the room. "We've put a few of Lark's things on her dresser," she says. "Tiny things she collected or wore. Please choose something you'd like to keep."

Very neatly arranged on the dresser with the marble top arc Lark's hair ribbons and charms, bracelets strung with glass beads or woven from embroidery thread, a tiny pink jewelry box shaped like a heart, silver rings with mother-of-pearl and turquoise, a silk butterfly for her hair, a necklace with one half of a broken heart. On the other end of her dresser is the collection of tiny porcelain animals she's had since she was little. None is bigger than a thimble. There's a tiny pony on its hind legs, a line of ducklings, a pink-and-gray pig, a tiger, and an elephant. At the end are two yellow birds with gray wings and black faces.

Larks . . . , I realize, and I go back to the day when we were very little and she showed me a picture of a lark in a book of birds. We were in the study, which always felt like a grandfather's room because it was filled with comfy old furniture. A granny-square afghan was spread over the back of the sofa. It felt so safe to be surrounded by oak walls and books, the sound of the dryer in the background, shafts of sunlight falling through the window.

I pick up one of the birds and touch the curve of

the feathers with my finger. Its beak is open. Singing. Nyetta has joined me at the far end of the dresser.

"I'm choosing this," she says, staring at the little bird resting in her palm.

"Me, too," I say.

She lifts her head and looks at me. She's tiny with dark circles under her eyes like she's either sick or can't sleep. She tilts her head so she can see me from the corner of her eye.

"She used to visit me."

Off to the side, Lark's friends are talking softly and looking over her things on the dresser. Everyone is delicate and well mannered, like we're each playing a role. I look at Nyetta in her dark dress and stockings, not sure if I've heard her right.

"She wanted me to see her . . . where the knife went in. But I couldn't." She looks down at the floor like she's ashamed. "I was too scared. The knife went in here," she says, pointing to her side. "It went between her ribs."

She's matter-of-fact about it, which frightens me more. I don't know what to say, but it seems best to take her seriously.

"When's the last time you saw her?" I ask.

"Three nights ago," she says, "but she won't come back. She's mad at me."

The little bird is in my pocket. It's so tiny I can close my hand without touching it. Nyetta balances hers in the palm of her hand. She bounces it slightly, like she's encouraging it to fly. She's rapt in the gesture, and for a moment she looks like any imaginative girl you might see.

"Go on, Lark," she says. "Eve will help you. She won't let you get trapped in that tree."

24. *Lark*

Roots snare my feet, pull my legs to the taproot. I try calling the three sisters for help, but my pulse is too weak. They watch me from their own trees, crying as I'm pulled deeper into the tree. The tree twists my arms into branches, encases me with heartwood and sap. The wound in my side hardens and scars, an ugly burl in the trunk.

My pulse snags. I'm static and fixed, scarred with the buds of fallen leaves, forced to look at the place where I died. Under the bark, my heart still throbs.

25. Nyetta

The doorbell rings. It's Eve and some boy about six feet tall, carrying a white pastry box.

"Hi," says Eve. I didn't notice her eyelashes the other night. She doesn't have many, but each one is perfectly pointed like the ends of a star. I stare at her so hard she has to take a step back.

"We brought you cupcakes," says the boy,

offering me the box.

"You went to Heidelberg," I say. "My favorite bakery." I look longingly at the castle etched on the gold sticker. I used to think it was where the princess pricked her finger. Ian and Eve both wear navy blue peacoats with long Harry Potter scarves wrapped around their necks. They're standing so close, their arms are touching. I bet they can feel each other through their coats. "Come in," I say.

26. *Eve*

Nyetta takes us into the family room. She settles in a leather recliner shaped like the letter C. The walls are lined with floor-to-ceiling bookshelves filled with academic texts about antiquities and archaeology. It's the only family room I've ever seen without a TV. On the side table next to her, strands of rust-colored beads hang in a clear plastic box.

"They're mummy beads," she says "My mother bought them when she was still in college." She gestures toward the other display boxes encasing bronze and stone objects. "It was the first thing in her collection."

"Whoa!" says Ian. "They must be worth a lot of money!"

"Not really," says Nyetta. "They're not as rare as you'd think."

She's quiet and composed, undisturbed by silence, content to answer my questions in a few words without asking any of her own.

"So . . ." I try again. "Do you play any sports? Take any lessons?"

"No," she says, staring back. Her eyes are dark shiny brown like espresso beans. "I don't even go to school anymore."

"Why not?" I ask.

Nyetta sighs. "My mother teaches me better.

Besides, I'm too tired. I can never get enough sleep."

Ian opens the pastry box and sends a shower of sprinkles to the floor. Nyetta jumps out of her chair

"Why did you do that?" she demands. "We can't eat those here! We never eat in this room!"

Ian picks up the sprinkles one by one, then we follow Nyetta to the breakfast room, where we pass around the box of cupcakes and begin to eat. Nyetta's mom pours tall glasses of milk and leaves. We sit at a yellow Formica table, silently eating. Nyetta chooses the chocolate truffle cupcake. She licks at the frosting like a cat. I choose the cupcake with the lost sprinkles. Ian makes half of his red velvet cupcake disappear in one bite.

"I've been thinking about what you told me at Lark's house. About how she used to visit you because she wanted you to see . . ."

"I can't talk about that here," whispers Nyetta.

"Why not?" I ask.

"*My mother*," she mouths, and twirls an index finger at the side of her temple. *"She'll go crazy."*

"Can we talk somewhere else?" whispers Ian.

Nyetta nods.

"Is there anyplace you want to go?" I ask.

"The Hello Kitty store," she says.

Between aisles of shelves filled with Hello Kitty pillows, alarm clocks, and stationery, Nyetta tells Ian how Lark used to visit her and now she doesn't anymore because she got fed up with her cowardice.

"Plus, she's almost a tree," she says. She talks about how girls can turn into trees if no one finds out what happened to them. "And it's not what they want. They hate being trees. All of them do. And there isn't much time before it happens to Lark. But I couldn't do it. So you and Eve have to. You got to see where the knife went in." She points to her left. "It went in here."

A giant plush Hello Kitty sits in the corner of

the store. She's dressed in a flowered kimono, surrounded by dozens of tiny clones. Nyetta sits in the huge white cat's lap and throws her arms around it. Ian takes a picture with his phone. "I'll email it to you," he says.

The jewelry counter glitters with Hello Kitty lockets, charm bracelets, and rings. I help Nyetta try on a pink watch. It blazes with crystals and has Hello Kitty faces instead of numbers. Tiny cats bob to and fro nodding yes.

"Twelve happy cats," says Ian.

Nyetta puts it up to her ear. "It has a good tick," she says.

She opens her purse, pulls out the different bills stuffed inside, and counts.

"Do you have enough?" I ask. "If not, I can lend you some."

She takes off the watch and gives it back to the salesperson.

"That's okay," she says, looking down at her clasped hands.

"I'm sure your mom would pay me back," I say.

"Let's go," she says. "I don't really want it."

TRIAL BEGINS FOR
FAIRFAX MAN ACCUSED OF
MURDERING ARLINGTON GIRL

◄O►

APRIL 10: Opening statements begin tomorrow in the trial of a Fairfax man accused of murdering Lark Austin, a 16-year-old Jefferson High School student.

Stephen Blaire, 29, is charged with kidnapping, assault, and first-degree murder. The girl was last seen the evening of January 23 in the lobby of the Virginia Gymnastics Academy, where she was waiting to be picked up by her father. She died in the early hours of January 24 of exposure, during the area's first major snowstorm. Two days later her body was found tied to a tree in

Potomac Overlook Park.

Arlington police say Blaire abducted the girl at knifepoint after luring her into his car at approximately 7:30 p.m. on January 23. He then drove her to Potomac Overlook Park, where he beat, stabbed, and sexually assaulted her. Prosecutors claim strong forensic evidence proves Blaire's guilt.

The trial is expected to last three or four days.

First-degree murder and sexual assault carry a mandatory life sentence in the state of Virginia.

27. *Lark*

heartwood sap beat pulse
taproot crown beat pulse leaf bark beat
pulse root sapwood beat pulse heartwood
sap beat pulse taproot crown beat pulse
leaf bark beat pulse root sapwood beat pulse
heartwood sap beat pulse taproot crown

beat pulse leaf bark beat pulse root sapwood beat
pulse heartwood sap beat pulse taproot
crown beat pulse leaf bark beat pulse root
sapwood beat pulse heartwood sap beat pulse
root crown beat pulse leaf bark beat pulse
root sapwood beat pulse heartwood sap
beat pulse taproot crown beat pulse
leaf bark beat pulse root sapwood beat pulse
heartwood sap beat pulse taproot crown beat
pulse leaf bark beat pulse root sapwood
beat pulse heartwood sap beat pulse taproot
crown beat pulse leaf bark beat pulse root
sapwood beat pulse heartwood sap beat pulse
taproot crown beat pulse leaf bark beat pulse
root sapwood heartwood sap beat pulse
taproot crown beat pulse leaf bark beat

pulse root sapwood beat pulse heartwood
sap beat pulse taproot crown beat pulse
leaf bark beat pulse root sapwood beat pulse
heartwood sap beat pulse taproot crown
beat pulse leaf bark beat pulse root sapwood beat
pulse heartwood sap beat pulse taproot
crown beat pulse leaf bark beat pulse root
sapwood beat pulse heartwood sap beat pulse
root crown beat pulse leaf bark beat pulse
root sapwood beat pulse heartwood sap
beat pulse taproot crown beat pulse
leaf bark beat pulse root sapwood beat pulse
heartwood sap beat pulse taproot crown beat
pulse leaf bark beat pulse root sapwood beat
pulse heartwood sap beat pulse taproot crown
beat pulse leaf bark beat pulse root sapwood

28. *Nyetta*

For once my mom drives me to Hallie's instead of having my dad get me. She even walks me up to the house and says hello to Zeke when he opens the door.

"Oh, hi," says Hallie, smiling as she bounds down the stairs. She's in another yoga outfit. Lavender and pink. The gold Buddha dances on her necklace. Her curls bounce.

"Hello," my mother answers. She's professional and polite. Short hair and trousers. Black turtleneck. Practical watch. It's April, and she's wearing sunglasses. I can't believe my father married both of these women. I've seen pictures of the weddings. My mom and dad in a church. Hallie and my dad in someone's backyard. My mother didn't want me to go. She said it would be too much for me. Anders and Zeke were the ring bearers. Hallie didn't wear white, but I guess that's because she was married before. Her first husband died.

Hallie tells Zeke to take my overnight bag to "Nyetta's room," and I can feel my mother tense up. She's sending out electrical impulses only I can read. *She's my daughter! My daughter! She doesn't have a room in your house!*

"Enjoy the weekend," she tells me.

"Thanks for driving," says Hallie. "And don't forget Sunday dinner! See you at six!"

The door slams and my mother stamps to the street. Her car takes off.

"Sunday dinner?" I ask, stunned. "All of us?"

"Yes. Sunday dinner. Family dinner."

"But we aren't a family," I say.

"Sure we are," says Hallie. "I'm making polenta."

I drift about the house, wondering where Hallie got such a weird idea and when my dad will be back from the store, feeling as tired as I've ever been in my whole life. I fall into the fluffy couch in front of the big-screen TV. Pillows pin me down like sandbags. The Disney Channel blares. Anders and Zeke sit directly in front of the screen, cross-legged, transfixed by lemurs and spider monkeys. Hallie sets up a little table for me with a cup of tea and a plate of gingersnaps.

"I want some!" Anders yells.

"Use your manners and I'll see."

"Nyetta didn't use her manners," says Zeke. "She

didn't even ask for cookies."

"Nyetta's tired," says Hallie. "She's been through a lot."

"Lucky!" says Zeke.

"No," says Hallie. "Not lucky." She puts her hand on my forehead, slides it to my cheek, checking for fever. "But things are getting better. I can feel it."

29. *Eve*

Inside the courtroom, fluorescent lights glare from the dropped white ceiling. I blink to refocus, trying to make out the faces of the jury in the blur. Lawyers scribble notes and tap on their laptops. They take out papers from one file and shuffle them into another. The jury seems tired. They swivel in their chairs or stare at the ceiling. The judge looks on, his chin propped up with his hand, his body swallowed in his black robe.

Ian holds my hand while the prosecutor opens his case. He tells the jury about the fibers found in Blaire's apartment and car and how they match those found on Lark's clothes.

"And that's not all," he tells the jury. He paces and gestures, drops his head for dramatic effect. "DNA evidence links Lark's blood to a knife found in his apartment, the very knife that he used to stab her here. . . ."

The lawyer taps the left side of his chest, the same place where Nyetta says Lark was stabbed, where Nyetta said the wound is, the one she had to see so Lark wouldn't turn into a tree. I shudder and feel sick. Ian and I turn to each other. It's true. What Nyetta told us is true.

We stay all day, listening to details of Lark's death, how the knife collapsed her lung, how semen was found on her leg, how her body entered hypothermia stage two, how her skin turned puffy and blue in stage three, how it took hours to die.

I listen to everything, storing facts in one corner of my brain while another remembers the last time I saw her alive, lumbering up her driveway days before she died. I was upstairs in my room, drawing windmills and empty fields, lonely farmhouses, canals lined with bare trees. A landscape I don't even know.

LarkLarkLarkLarkLarkLarkLarkLarkLark . . .

Her name pulses in my head like a heartbeat. Memories and images fall into slots. I see her pour her body into a perfect back dive, entering the clear blue water with barely a splash. I see our footprints in the mud, her damp hair hanging down her back as she runs in front of me. Smells of sunscreen and cut grass waft through the woods. Only a few feet away was where she would die.

* * *

Days later, after the evidence, the testimonies, the witnesses, and the questions, after the closing arguments and the guilty verdict, I take Ian to the place in the woods where Lark and I used to throw stones at the islands. Thousands and thousands of tight little buds burst above us on silvery branches. Here and there, between outcroppings of rock, bright shoots sprout, bold and insistent. We wander the woods, trying to find the exact tree where she died. We place our hands on one after another, feeling deep into the tiny ridges of bark for her pulse.

"Here!" calls Ian.

A tall elm clings to bare rock. Roots snake between stone and bury themselves deep in the earth. I put my hands next to his.

"Look," he says.

I peer into the bark and there she is, her face through the wood. She's startled and fraught, like she's been grabbed by the hair or caught in a trap.

Her eyes stare into mine. Her breath rasps. Her heart beats faint and fast beneath my hands.

"We know, Lark," I say. "Let go of Nyetta. Let us be the ones to set you free."

30. *Lark*

Go! urge the dead girls, but the tree pulls my hair, branches pluck, tear my skin. Sap stings my eyes. I am almost smothered by the tree's amber core, its dark heart, its taproot drinking minerals.

She loves you, say the dead girls. *You didn't know.*

And I didn't, but now she puts her palms on my face, looks long at the wound in my side. She and Ian offer their hands. I reach through growth rings. My hand breaks through the bark to grasp theirs, holding on tight while they pull me back into the world. The earth is soft, almost warm. Birds sing and scatter across the tin sky.

"Remember," asks Eve, "our footprints in the mud?"

Words overlap, clutter my mouth. I can't speak, but if I could I would say, "Eve, my friend."

31. Nyetta

"Are you sure you want to do this?" my mother asks.

"Yes!" I say. "Yes. Yes. Yes."

She crinkles her forehead. She thinks the ritual Eve and I made up is too morbid. She wonders if I might crack up or go crazy and start talking to ghosts again. If only she knew what I almost did. She should make an appointment with April, then talk to

Hallie, who thinks the plan sounds great because she understands these things, for all her yoga and rose quartz, and weaving and baking bread. I think she must know about trees and girls. Someday I will ask.

My mom's still unsure about letting me kayak to the Three Sisters with Ian and Eve. I use the words April gave me to help convince her it will be a "good experience."

"It's my way of saying good-bye. Of honoring Lark and letting her go. She would like this. And remember . . . Ian's on the crew team and he practices on the river all the time. And he's a Red Cross lifeguard. And Eve will be there, too. And we'll all wear life jackets, of course. And don't forget I can swim."

She disappears into her office, closing the door. I huddle against the wall in my room, listening. She's dialing the handheld, and I can tell by the rhythm she's calling my dad's cell. For some reason they've decided to act like friends. I've even heard her ask about Hallie and the boys. Her voice is too soft to hear, but in a few minutes she hangs up and comes into my room.

"Okay," she says, "you can go. But I'm going to drive you there and wait on the dock until you come back."

Finally it's Saturday, and we drive to the boathouse, the old-fashioned one with the dark green shutters, the one you can see under the arches of Key Bridge.

I run through the boathouse, sending echoes. Paddles and oars, dinghies and rowboats, sloops and canoes hang on the walls and rest on old planks of wood. Outside, the sun pours down on the dock. It creaks and groans when I step on it.

"There they are," says my mother.

My hand shoots up to wave at Eve and Ian. They're carrying a sleek silver kayak to the end of the dock.

My mom makes us eat a snack before we go. She's made sandwiches and pours little cups of hot chocolate from a thermos. We stand in a circle, taking little sips. "You aren't going near Great Falls, are you?"

"Not at all," laughs Ian. "It's going to be an easy trip. There's hardly any current today. No wind. Look how flat the water is!"

He points to the river. Diamonds of light speckle the surface. The trees on the Virginia side are bright green with new leaves. Weeping willows bend over boulders and lean to the river.

Ian sets the kayak in the water, holding it steady while Eve and I step in. Then he pushes us off and slips in behind me, and we're off, paddling in sync, making our way downstream. I've never been in a kayak, never been so low in the water before. I can touch the top and peer down to the muddy bottom. Dark birds with bright eyes, mallards and geese, float between rushes. They're too scared to come near us but too curious to fly away. Blade-shaped grasses undulate in eddies. Clouds of gold silt flash and disappear. Sometimes I see rotting trees at the river bottom, their roots draped with filmy green algae. If I happened to touch it, I think I might faint.

"I would hate to go swimming here," I say.

"No way," says Ian. "Not here. But farther down, there's a great swimming hole with deep, clear water and a little beach off to the side."

We paddle along, pulled by the current to the Three Sisters. They're bigger than I thought; rockier, too. The river laps against the islands and swirls. Ian steers us to the middle island, the one with the scraggly tree. He jumps out with a lead of rope that he ties to a branch that's wedged between boulders. Eve jumps out next, then the two of them give me a hand to help me find my footing. We scramble along, sliding our hands between cracks in the rock and pulling ourselves up. When we're at the top, I get that same unattached, airy feeling like when you're standing on top of the roof of a car. All around me are the sounds of the river.

Eve opens her hand, and there's the little china bird, the lark with the open mouth, singing. I pull mine out of my pocket, the one with the outstretched wings. The roots of the maple tree spread over the rock and spill into the cracks. They're dappled with lichen and moss like the boulders they cling to.

"I'll put mine here," says Eve, and she rests it on a pillow of moss. I put mine next to it.

Maybe they'll stay there for years and years. Maybe they'll leave with the wind or the storm. Lark can choose. She's watching. She's happy to see her little birds are there.

Acknowledgments

Many thanks to Lori Newsome, Celia Leckey, Carla Johnson Boucher, Tory Sievers, Joanna Cotler, Laura Geringer, Kim Merrill, Maria Alden, Francesca Lia Block, Sofie Fier, and Susie Terasaki.